"Are you thinking about **how it would** **feel like if my mouth was to touch yours right now?"**

Angel's gaze flew up and clashed with pure molten gold heat. An answering heat invaded her lower body, and she felt the urge to clamp her legs together, as if that might dampen the strange ache building up there.

Before she could articulate a response, his hand had cupped her jaw and cheek, and suddenly there was no distance between them—only him, so tall and close that he blocked out the sky. And his head was descending, coming nearer and nearer. He smelled musky and *hot*. It was something so earthy that Angel could feel the response being tugged from her down low in her belly, as if she recognized it on some primitive level. Dimly she wondered if this was what people meant when they talked about animal attraction.

Desperately trying to cling to something, *anything* rational, Angel brought a hand to cover his, to pull it down, to stop him, to say no…. But then his mouth was so close that she could feel his breath feather there, mingling with hers. Her mouth tingled. She wanted…she wanted—

All about the author…
Abby Green

ABBY GREEN deferred doing a social anthropology degree to work freelance as an assistant director in the film and TV industry—which is a social study in itself! Since then it's been early starts, long hours, mucky fields, ugly car parks and wet-weather gear—especially working in Ireland. She has no bona fide qualifications, but after years of dealing with recalcitrant actors she could probably help negotiate a peace agreement between two warring countries. After discovering a guide to writing romance, she decided to capitalize on her longtime love for Harlequin® romances and attempt to follow in the footsteps of such authors as Kate Walker and Penny Jordan. She's enjoying the excuse to be paid to sit inside, away from the elements. She lives in Dublin and hopes that you will enjoy her stories. You can e-mail her at abbygreen3@yahoo.co.uk.

Abby Green

THE VIRGIN'S SECRET

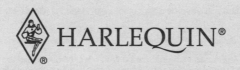

TORONTO • NEW YORK • LONDON
AMSTERDAM • PARIS • SYDNEY • HAMBURG
STOCKHOLM • ATHENS • TOKYO • MILAN • MADRID
PRAGUE • WARSAW • BUDAPEST • AUCKLAND

Recycling programs
for this product may
not exist in your area.

ISBN-13: 978-0-373-23696-1

THE VIRGIN'S SECRET

First North American Publication 2010.

Copyright © 2010 by Abby Green.

This edition published by arrangement with Harlequin Books S.A.

For questions and comments about the quality of this book please contact us at Customer_eCare@Harlequin.ca.

® and TM are trademarks of the publisher. Trademarks indicated with ® are registered in the United States Patent and Trademark Office, the Canadian Trade Marks Office and in other countries.

www.eHarlequin.com

Printed in U.S.A.

THE VIRGIN'S SECRET

This is for my lovely editor, Meg,
who shines a torchlight into the dark corners
where I've tied myself into knots, and helps me
unravel it all again into something coherent.
Thanks for everything—you're a star.

I'd also like to dedicate this book with
special thanks to Anne Mary Luttrell,
whose waiting room is a magical place
where many a plot has been incubated.
Thanks for your healing hands (needles) and words.

PROLOGUE

LEONIDAS PARNASSUS looked out of the window of his private plane. They'd just landed at Athens airport. To his utter consternation his chest felt tight and constricted—a sensation he didn't welcome. He was curiously reluctant to move from his seat, even though the cabin staff were preparing to open the door, even though sitting still and not moving was anathema to him. He told himself it was because he was still chafing at the reality that he'd acquiesced to his father's demand that he come to Athens for 'talks'.

Leo Parnassus did not carve out time for anything or anyone he deemed a waste of his resources and energy. Not a business venture, a lover, nor a father who had put building up the family fortune and clearing their shamed name before a relationship with his son. Leo grimaced slightly, his face so harsh that the steward who had been approaching him stopped abruptly and hovered uncertainly. Leo saw nothing though but the heat haze on the tarmac outside and the darkness of his own thoughts.

He was Greek through and through, and yet he'd never set foot on Greek soil. His family had been exiled from their ancestral home before he was born, but his father had returned triumphantly just a few years ago; finally realising a lifelong dream to clear their name of a terrible crime and to glory in their new-found status and inestimable wealth.

Bitter anger rose when Leo remembered his beloved *ya ya*'s lined and worn face. The sadness that had grooved deep lines around her mouth and shadowed her eyes. It had been too late for *her* to return home. She'd died in an alien country she'd never grown to love. Even though his grandmother had urged him to return as soon as he'd had the chance, he'd condemned Athens on her behalf for breaking her heart. He'd always sworn that he wouldn't return to the place that had spurned his family so easily.

Athens was still home to the Kassianides family who had been responsible for all that pain and sadness, and who were suffering far too belatedly and minutely for what they had done. They had cast a long shadow over his childhood which had been indelibly marked by their actions, in so many ways.

And yet, despite all that…here he was. Because

something in his father's voice, an unmistakable weakness had called to him, in spite of everything that had happened. It had touched him on some level. In short, he'd felt *compelled* to come. Perhaps he wanted to prove to himself that he was not at the mercy of his emotions?

The very thought of that made him go cold; at the tender age of eight he'd made an inarticulate vow never to let any intensity of emotion overwhelm him, because that's what had killed his mother. Surely he could handle looking his ancestral home in the face and turn his back on it once and for all? Of course he could.

But first he had to deal with the fact that his father wanted him to take over the Parnassus shipping business. Leo had denied his inheritance a long time ago; he'd embraced the entrepreneurial American spirit, and now ran a diverse subsidiary business that encompassed finance, acquisitions, and real estate, recently snapping up an entire block of buildings in New York's Lower East Side for redevelopment.

His sole input to his father's business had been a couple of years before when they'd tightened the noose of revenge around the neck of Tito Kassianides, the last remaining patriarch of the Kassianides family. It was the one thing that had joined father and son: a united desire to seek vengeance.

Leo had taken singular pleasure in making sure that the Kassianides' demise was ensured, thanks to a huge merger his father had orchestrated with Aristotle Levakis, one of Greece's titans of industry. That victory now, though, when he was faced with the reality of touching down in Greece, felt curiously empty. He couldn't help but think of his grandmother, how much she'd longed for this moment and never got a chance to see it.

A discreet cough sounded, 'I'm sorry, sir?'

Leo looked up, intensely irritated to have been observed in a private moment. He saw the steward was gesturing to the now open cabin door. Leo's chest clenched tightly again, and he had the childishly bizarre urge to tell them to slam the door shut and take off, back to New York. It was almost as if something outside that door lay in wait for him. Such a mix of emotions was rising to the surface, and it was so unwelcome that he stood up jerkily from his seat as if he could shake them off.

He walked to the cabin door, very aware of the eyes of his staff on him. Normally it didn't bother him, he was used to people looking at him for his reaction, but now it scraped over his skin like sandpaper.

The heat hit him first, dry and searing. Strangely familiar. He breathed in the Athens air for the first time in his life and felt his heart hit hard with the intensifying of that absurd feeling of familiarity. He'd always felt that coming here would feel like betraying his grandmother's memory, but now it was as if she was behind him, gently pushing him forward. For a man who lived by cool logic and intellect, it was an alien and deeply disturbing sensation.

He concealed his eyes behind dark shades as an ominous prickling skated over his skin. He had the very unwelcome sensation that everything in his life was about to change.

At the same moment on the other side of Athens.

'Delphi, just take a deep breath and tell me what's wrong—I can't help you until I know what it is.'

That just provoked more weeping. Angel grabbed another tissue, a trickle of unease going down her spine now. Her younger half-sister said brokenly, 'I don't do this kind of thing, Angel, I'm a law student!'

Angel smoothed her pretty sister's fall of mahogany hair behind one ear and said soothingly, 'I know, sweetie. Look, it can't be that bad, whatever it is, so just tell me and then we can deal with it.'

Angel was absolutely confident when she said this. Delphi was introverted, too quiet. She always had been, and even more so since a tragic accident had killed her twin sister about six years ago. Ever since then she'd buried herself in books and studies, so when she said quietly, after a little sniffly hiccup, '*I'm pregnant…*' the words simply didn't register in Angel's head.

They didn't register until Delphi spoke again, with a catch in her voice.

'Angel—did you hear me? I'm pregnant. That's what… that's what's wrong.'

Angel's hands tightened reflexively around her half-sister's and she looked into her dark brown eyes—so different from her own light blue ones, even though they both shared the same father.

Angel tried not to let the shock suck her under. 'Delph, how did it happen?' She grimaced. 'I mean, I know *how*…but…'

Her sister looked down guiltily, a flush staining her cheeks red. 'Well…you know Stavros and I have been getting more serious…' Delphi looked up again, and Angel's heart melted at the turmoil she saw on her sister's face.

'We both wanted to, Angel. We felt the time was right and we wanted it to be with someone we loved…'

Angel's heart constricted. That was exactly what she had wanted too, right up until— Her sister continued, cutting through Angel's painful memory.

'And we were careful, we used protection, but it…' She blushed again, obviously mortified to have to be talking about this at all. 'It split. We decided to wait until we knew there was something to worry about…and now there is.'

'Does Stavros know?'

Delphi nodded miserably and looked sheepish. 'I never told you this, but on my birthday last month Stavros asked me to marry him.'

Angel wasn't that surprised; she'd suspected something like this might happen with the two of them. They'd been sweethearts for ever. 'Has he spoken to his parents?'

Delphi nodded, but fresh tears welled. 'His father has told him that if we marry he'll be disinherited. You know they've never liked us…'

Angel winced inwardly for her sister. Stavros came from one of the oldest and most established families in Greece, and his parents were inveterate snobs. But before she could say anything Delphi was continuing in a choked voice.

'…and now it's worse, because the Parnassus family are home, and everyone knows what happened, and with Father going bankrupt…' she trailed off miserably.

A familiar feeling of shame gripped Angel at the mention of that name: *Parnassus*. Many years before, her family had committed a terrible crime against the much poorer Parnassus family, falsely accusing them of a horrific murder. It was only recently that they had atoned for that transgression. When her great-uncle Costas, who had actually committed the crime, had confessed all in a suicide note, the Parnassus family, who were now phenomenally successful and wealthy, had seen their chance for revenge, and had returned to Athens from America on a wave of glory. The consequent scandal and shake-up in power meant that her father, Tito Kassianides, had started haemorrhaging business and money, to the point that they now faced certain bankruptcy. Parnassus had made certain that everyone now knew how the Kassianides family had wilfully abused their power in the most heinous way.

'Stavros wants us to elope—'

Angel's focus came back, and she immediately went to interject, but Delphi put up a hand, her pale face streaked with tears. 'But I won't allow him to do that.'

Angel shut her mouth again.

'I won't be responsible for him being cut off and disinherited—not when I know how important it is to him that he gets into politics some day. This could ruin all his chances.'

Angel marvelled at her sweet sister's selflessness. She took her hands again and said gently, 'And what about you, Delph? You deserve some happiness too, and you deserve a father for your baby.'

A door slammed downstairs and they both flinched minutely.

'He's home...' Delphi breathed, a mixture of fear and loathing in her voice as the inarticulate roars of their father's drunken rage drifted up the stairs. More tears welled in her red-rimmed eyes, and suddenly Angel was extremely aware of the fact that her baby sister was now pregnant and needed at all costs to be protected from the potential pain of dealing with any scandal or losing Stavros. She took her gently by the shoulders and forced her to look into her eyes.

'Sweetheart, you did the right thing telling me. Just act as if everything is normal and we'll work something out. It'll be fine—'

Delphi's voice took on a hysterical edge. 'But Father is getting more and more out of control, and mother is unravelling at the seams—'

'Shh. Look, haven't I always been there for you?'

Angel winced inwardly. She *hadn't* been there when Delphi had needed her most, after Damia, her twin's death, and that was why she'd made the promise to stay at home until Delphi gained her own independence, her twin's death having affected her profoundly. Now her sister just nodded tearily, biting her lip, and looked at Angel with such nakedly trusting eyes that Angel had to batten down the almost overwhelming feeling of panic. She caught a lone tear falling down Delphi's face and wiped it away gently with a thumb.

'You've got exams coming up in a few months, and enough to be thinking about now. Just leave everything to me.'

Her sister flung skinny arms around Angel's neck, hugging her tight. Angel hugged her back, emotion coursing through her to think that in a few months her sister's belly would be swollen with a baby. She had to make sure she and Stavros got married. Delphi wasn't hardy and cocky, as her twin had been. Where one had been effervescent and exuberant, the other had always been the more quiet foil. And as for their father—if he found out—

Delphi pulled back and spoke Angel's thoughts out loud. 'What if Father—?'

Angel cut her off. 'He won't. I promise. Now, why don't you go to bed and get some sleep? And don't worry, I'll handle it.'

CHAPTER ONE

I'LL handle it. Those fatalistic words still reverberated in Angel's head a week later. She'd gone to speak with Stavros' father herself, to try and remonstrate with him, but he hadn't even deigned to see her. It couldn't have been made clearer that they were social outcasts.

'*Kassianides!*'

Abruptly Angel was pulled out of her spiralling black thoughts when her boss called her name. It must have been the second or third time, judging by the impatience on his face.

'When you can join us back on earth, go down to the pool and make sure it's completely clear and that the tea lights are set out on the tables.'

She stuttered an apology and fled. In all honesty Angel's preoccupation had been distracting her from something much more panic-inducing and stressful. Almost too stressful to contemplate.

She was here at the Parnassus villa, high in the

hills of Athens, to waitress at a party that was being thrown for Leonidas Parnassus, the son of Georgios Parnassus. Everyone was buzzing about the fact that he might be about to take over the family business and what a coup it would be, Leo Parnassus having become a multimillionaire entrepreneur in his own right.

It hit her again as she hurried down the steps that were expertly overgrown with extravagantly flowering bougainvillea. *She was in the Parnassus villa, the home of the family who hated hers with a passion.*

For a second she stopped in her tracks, a hand going to her breast as an intense pain tightened in her chest. This was the absolute worst place she could be in the world. For a second she felt hysteria rising at the irony of it. She, Angel Kassianides, was about to serve drinks to the *crème de la crème* of Athens, right under the Parnassuses nose. The thought of what her father would do if he could see her now made her break out in a cold sweat.

She bit her lip and forced herself to go on, breathing a sigh of relief when she had a quick look around the pool area and saw no one. The guests hadn't started to arrive yet and, though there were some staying at the villa, Angel knew that they'd be getting ready. There was no reason for anyone to be by the pool, but still…an uneasy prickling skated over her skin.

She hadn't been able to avoid coming here tonight. She and her waiter colleagues had been halfway to their secret destination in a packed minibus before it had been revealed, for 'security reasons'. Angel knew well that if she'd bailed out of this evening her boss would have sacked her on the spot. He'd sacked people for less in his pre-stigious catering company. She couldn't afford for that to happen—not when her income was the only thing helping put her sister through college and keeping food on their table.

She tried to reassure herself: her boss was English, recently moved to Athens with his English/Greek wife. He knew nothing of the sig-nificance of who Angel was, nor her scandalous connection to the Parnassus family. She busied herself placing out the tea lights in their antique silver holders in the middle of the white damask-covered tables, and sent up fervent thanks that, tonight of all nights, not one of the other staff were local. Things were so busy at the moment that her boss had had to call in their part-time workers, and they were all either foreign or from outside Athens.

Her only fear now was that someone at the party might recognise her. But, knowing these people as she did, she'd no doubt that in her uniform of black skirt and white shirt they'd not take a second look at her. She worried her lip again. Perhaps she could just stay in the kitchen and get the trays together and avoid—

Angel started suddenly when she heard the splash of water coming from nearby. *Someone was in the pool*. Carefully she placed the last candle down and made to slip away, back up to the kitchen. As if she'd been subliminally aware of it but had blocked it out, she realised that someone must have been in the pool all along—but not swimming, so she hadn't noticed them.

The sky was a dusky violet colour, so perhaps that was also why she hadn't—Angel glanced quickly to her right as a flash of movement caught her eye, and her legs stopped functioning when the sight before her registered on her retina and in her brain.

An olive-skinned Greek god was hauling himself in one powerfully sleek move out of the water, droplets of water cascading off taut muscles. Everything seemed to go into slow motion as the sheer height and breadth of him was revealed. Angel shook her head stupidly, but it felt as if it had been stuffed with cotton wool. Greek gods didn't exist. This was a man, a flesh-and-blood man. And the minute she registered that she was standing transfixed, staring at him, she panicked.

But her body wouldn't obey her order to move, or it would, but her limbs all moved in independent directions, and to her utter horror she found herself backing into a poolside chair and almost toppling over it. And she would have, if the man hadn't moved like lightning and grabbed her, so that instead of falling back she fell forward into his chest, with his hands around her upper arms.

For a long moment Angel tried to tell herself that this wasn't happening. That she wasn't breathing in an intoxicating mix of spice and earthiness. That she wasn't all but plastered against a bare, *wet* chest which felt as hard as steel, her lips just a breath away from pressing against skin covered in a light dusting of intensely masculine hair.

Angel tried to break away, and pulled back, forcing his hands to drop. Heat scorched upwards over her cheeks as she finally stood upright again and found her eyes level with hard, flat brown nipples. She looked up, swallowing, and her gaze skittered up and past broad shoulders to his face.

'I'm so sorry. I just…got startled. The light… I didn't see…'

The man quirked an ebony brow. Angel swallowed again. Lord, but his face was as beautiful as the rest of him. Not beautiful, she amended, that was too girly a word. He was devastating. Thick black hair lay sleek against his head, and high cheekbones offset an impossibly hard jaw. His mouth was forbidding, but held a promise of sensuality that resonated deep in her body.

Suddenly that mouth stopped being forbidding and quirked. She nearly had to put out a hand again to steady herself. A thin scar ran from his upper lip to his nose, making her fight the absurd urge to reach up and trace it. Making her wonder how he'd got it—this complete stranger!

'Are you okay?'

Angel nodded vaguely. He sounded American; perhaps he was a business colleague, a guest who was staying over. Although somehow, in her muddled brain, that didn't fit either. He was *someone*. She struggled to remember where she was, what she was here to do. *Who* she was.

She nodded. 'I'm…I'm fine.'

He frowned slightly, seemingly completely at ease with his lack of dress. 'You're not Greek?'

Angel alternately shook and nodded her head. 'I am Greek. But I'm also half-Irish. I spent a lot of time in boarding school there…so my accent is more neutral.' She clamped her mouth shut. What was she blathering on about?

The man frowned a little deeper, his glance up and down taking in her uniform. 'And yet you're waitressing here?'

The incredulity in his tone made Angel's sanity rush back. Only girls from privileged backgrounds in Greece went abroad for schooling. Immediately she felt vulnerable. She was meant to be fading into the background, not engaging in conversation with the guests of the hosts.

She backed away, looking somewhere in the region of his shoulder. 'Please excuse me. I have to get back to work.'

She was about to turn when she heard him drawl laconically, 'You might want to dry off before you start handing out champagne.'

Angel followed his gaze down to where it rested on her chest. On her breasts. She gasped when she saw that she was indeed drenched, her shirt opaque and her plain white bra clearly visible, along with two very pointedly hard nipples. How long had she been plastered against him like some mindless groupie?

With a strangled gasp of mortification Angel scrambled backwards, nearly tripping over a chair again and only just righting it and herself before there could be a repeat rescue performance. All she heard as she fled back up the steps was a mocking, deep-throated chuckle.

* * *

A little later, Leonidas Parnassus looked around the thronged salon and tried to stifle his irritation when he couldn't see the waitress. It had made him uncomfortable, how urgent his need to see her again had been as soon as he'd walked into the main reception room. It had also made him uncomfortable how vividly her image had come back to him in his recent shower, forcing him to turn the temperature to cold.

And now her image surged back again, mocking his attempts to thrust it aside. He recalled how she'd looked, with a dark flush on her cheeks, those intensely light blue eyes wide and ringed with thick black lashes, staring at him like a startled fawn. As if she'd never seen a man before.

She had a tiny beauty spot just on the edge of a full lower lip, and he grimaced when he felt the effect remembering that had on his lower body. He hated having such an arbitrary response. But when he'd seen her arrive by the pool and do her work, with quick, economic movements, her glossy light brown hair pulled into a high topknot, something about her had stirred him. Something about her intense preoccupation, for patently she hadn't noticed him in the pool. And Leo was not a man who was used to going unnoticed.

When he'd caught her against him in that completely instinctive move tendrils of her hair had come free and framed her face and the defined line of her jaw, making him want to slip his hand into the glossy strands and cause it to fall down around her shoulders. He could almost feel it over his hands now, the heavy silky weight.

Irritation spiked again. Where was she? Had she been a figment of his imagination? His father approached then, with a colleague, and Leo forced a benign smile to his mouth, hating the fact that he was in thrall to a nameless waitress.

Distracting him momentarily was the reality he now faced of just how frail his father had become, even since he'd seen him last. As if something within him had shifted subtly but profoundly. He felt a deep-seated sense of inevitability steal over him, he was needed here, his own empire not-withstanding. But *was* his place really here? He tried out the word now: *home*. His heart beat fast.

He thought of his sterile, yet state-of-the-art penthouse apartment in New York; the steel and silver skyscrapers of the world he inhabited. He thought of his impeccably groomed and very experienced blonde mistress; he thought of what it might be like to walk away from all of that—and he felt…nothing.

Athens, being here for the past week, had confounded his every expectation. He'd thought he'd feel nothing. On the contrary, he felt as though he'd been plugged into something deeply primal within his soul. Something had been brought to life, and wouldn't be pushed back to some dim and distant recess.

Just then, as if to compound this feeling, he caught sight of something in the far corner of the room. Glossy hair piled high, a long neck. A familiar slim back. Leo's heart started to thud, this time to a very different beat.

Angel was trying to keep her head down and not meet anyone's eye. She'd done her best to stay in the kitchen, preparing the trays, but her boss had eventually sent her up to the main salon as she was his most experienced staff member.

At that moment she caught a pointed frowning look from Aristotle Levakis across the room—he was business partner to Parnassus, and her stomach quivered with renewed panic. This was a disaster in the making. Aristotle Levakis knew her, because their fathers had been friendly before Aristotle's father had died. Angel could remember that Aristotle had been to one or two parties at her father's house over the years.

In the act of offering some red wine to a small group of people, she had to keep going, but then she got accidentally jostled by another waiter. The tray tipped off balance, and with mounting horror

Angel watched four glasses full of red wine disgorge their contents all over a beautiful woman's pristine and very white designer dress.

For a second nothing happened. The woman was just looking down at her dress, aghast. And then it came, her voice so shrill that Angel winced. Conversely, at the same time, an awful silence seemed to descend.

'You stupid, stupid girl—'

But then, just as suddenly, a huge dark shape appeared at Angel's side, and she barely had time to take in a breath before she registered that it was the man from the pool. Her heart skipped a beat, before starting again erratically. He sent her a quick wink before taking the gasping woman aside to speak to her in low, hushed tones, and Angel saw her boss hurry forward to take the matter in hand.

Her boss and the woman were summarily dispatched, and then the man turned around to face Angel. Words dropped into her head but made no sense. He was so downright intimidating in an exquisite tuxedo that shock was rendering her speechless, breathless and motionless.

He calmly took the now empty tray from her hand and passed it to another waiter. The mess from the fallen drinks was already being cleared up. Angel would have protested that she should look after it, if she could have spoken.

Everyone else in the immediate vicinity seemed to melt away, and with a light, yet commanding touch from his hand on her arm Angel felt herself being manoeuvred across the room, until they'd walked through a set of open patio doors and out to the blessed quiet of the grand terrace.

The cool and fragrant evening air curled around Angel like a caress, but she felt hot, right down to her very core. Hot from embarrassment and hot from where this man's big hand was curled around her upper arm. They came to a stop beside a low wall, beyond which a pristine lawn sloped gently downwards and off into the distance.

Silence surrounded them, thick and heavy, the muted sounds of the party coming from behind the closed patio doors. *Had he closed the doors?* The thought of him doing that to give them privacy made her shiver. She looked up, and with a disconcerting amount of effort pulled her arm free from his light, yet devastating grip. He smiled down at her, putting his hands in his pockets, and he looked so rakishly handsome that Angel felt weak all over again. Hair that had been slicked back with water was now thick and glossy, a little over-long.

'So…we meet again.'

Angel forced her brain to retain a small sliver

of sanity, but no matter how much she wanted it to, she feared her voice wouldn't come out as cool as she hoped for. 'I'm sorry…you must think me an awful klutz. I'm not normally so clumsy. Thank you for…' She gestured to the room, thinking of the red stain spreading over the woman's white dress again and feeling sick. 'For defusing the situation, but I don't think my boss will forgive me for it. That dress looked like it was worth about a year's worth of my wages.'

He took a hand out of his pocket and waved it nonchalantly. 'Consider it taken care of. I saw what happened, it was an accident.'

Angel gasped. 'I can't let you do a thing like that. I don't even know you.' His insouciance and casual display of wealth made something cold lodge in her chest. It was a rejection from deep within her of this whole social scene. She'd grown up with it and it reminded her too much of the darkness in her own family.

His eyes glinted with something dangerous. 'On the contrary, I'd say that we're well on the way to becoming…acquainted.'

An electric current seemed to spring into action in that moment. The man moved closer to Angel, closing the small distance between them, and the breath lodged in her throat. She couldn't think, couldn't speak. His eyes held hers, and for the second time that day she noted the way they seemed to burn with a golden light.

He lifted a hand and trailed his finger down one cheek to the delicate line of her jaw. It left a line of tingling fire in its wake.

'I haven't been able to stop thinking about you.'

The something cold that had lodged in Angel's chest melted. 'You…haven't?'

He shook his head. 'Or your mouth.'

'My mouth…' Angel repeated stupidly. Her gaze dropped to *his* mouth then, and she saw once again the jagged line of the scar extending from his upper lip. She had the strongest desire to reach up and trace it with a finger, so strong that she shook.

'Are you thinking about what it would feel like if my mouth was to touch yours right now?'

Angel's gaze flew up and clashed with pure molten golden heat. An answering heat invaded her lower body. She felt the urge to clamp her legs together, as if that might calm the disturbing ache building up there.

Before she could answer, or articulate a response, his hand had cupped her jaw and cheek, and suddenly there was no distance between them, only him, so tall and close that he blocked out the sky, and his head was descending, coming nearer and nearer.

He smelt musky and *hot*. It was something so

earthy that Angel could feel the response being tugged from down low in her belly, as if she recognised it on some primitive level. Dimly she wondered if this was what people meant when they talked about animal attraction.

Desperately trying to cling onto something, *anything* rational, Angel brought a hand up to cover his, to pull it down, to stop him, to say no… But then his mouth was so close that she could feel his breath feather there, mingling with hers. Her mouth tingled. She wanted…she wanted—

'Sir?'

Angel wanted his mouth on hers so badly that she made a telling move closer–

'Mr Parnassus…sir?'

Angel's eyes had been fluttering closed, but suddenly flew open again. Their mouths were just about touching. If Angel was to put out her tongue she'd be able to explore his lips, their shape and texture. And then the name that had just been uttered exploded into her consciousness properly.

Mr Parnassus.

Reality slammed back, and the cacophony of the party rushed out to meet them through open doors. Angel was barely aware of pulling his hand down and moving back. Shock was starting to spread through her entire body. Someone else came out to the patio then. The butler who had been standing there—*for how long?*—melted away discreetly. The new arrival was the host's wife, Olympia Parnassus. Angel knew this because she'd given all the waiting staff a pep talk in the kitchen earlier.

'Leo, darling, your father is looking for you, it's almost time for the speech.'

In a smooth move, Angel realised that she'd been effectively shielded from view. She felt more than heard the deep rumble of response.

'Give me two minutes here, Olympia.'

His tone was implacable. Clearly he was someone used to giving commands and having them met. He was *Leonidas Parnassus.*

Angel barely heard the older woman make some comment before she turned and clipped her way back into the party in her high heels, pulling the doors shut again. Shock was gathering force, and Angel started to react. She had to get out of here.

She knew that Leonidas Parnassus had turned back to face her, but she couldn't look at him. A warm hand tipped her chin up and she felt sick. She couldn't avoid his eyes unless she closed her own, and the thought of doing that made panic rise. He smiled a sexy smile.

'Please forgive the interruption. I'll have to go in a minute, but…where were we?'

Angel had to get out of here right *now*. She'd

just been about to kiss Leonidas Parnassus, the very man who must be gloating over her family's very public ruination. A sudden spurt of anger bloomed. They were in dire straits, and it was all because of *his* family and their lust for revenge. She thought of Delphi, who was so vulnerable now; she and her sister didn't deserve to be paying for something that had happened decades before.

Angel pulled down his hand and forced frost into her voice. 'Look, I don't know what you're playing at. I have to get back to work. if my boss saw me out here with you I'd be sacked on the spot, which is obviously something that hasn't occurred to you.'

Leonidas Parnassus looked at her for a long moment before straightening to his full intimidating height and moving back a pace. Gone was the sexily teasing man of just moments before and in his place now stood the son and heir of a vast fortune. The man who was already a self-made millionaire. No wonder she'd had that feeling earlier that he *was someone*.

Arrogant confidence oozed from every pore, and Angel had to repress a shiver at the cold of his eyes—not tawny gold any more, but almost black, like flint.

'Forgive me.' His voice was frigid. 'I would never have attempted to kiss you if I'd known you found the prospect so repugnant.'

His demeanour made a mockery of his words. He was completely unrepentant. At that moment he reached out and cupped her jaw again. Her heart hammered against her ribs, she felt herself flushing.

Any pretence of remorse was gone, or charm. 'Who do you think you're kidding, sweetheart? Don't ever fool yourself like that again. I know the signs of desire, and you're practically panting for me right now, just like you were by the pool.'

Angel ripped his hand down again, panic surging in earnest. If he had even an *inkling* of who she was… 'Don't be ridiculous. I am not. I want you to get out of my way, please, so I can get back to work.'

'I will,' he bit out. 'But not before we've proved your words to be a lie.'

Before Angel could take a breath he'd cupped her face in both his hands, stepped right up to her body, and his mouth was crashing down onto her shocked open one with all the force of a huge wave. Her hands covered his in a hazy attempt to remove them, and she struggled against the onslaught, but it felt like going against the strongest current.

Her open mouth had provided an unwitting invitation to his, and his tongue stabbed deep and plundered, seeking hers, sucking it deep. To be kissed so intimately shook her to her core.

Her body had stiffened with the shock of his

action, but a spreading, melting sensation was quickly taking over. The urge to fight was becoming more and more distant. All Angel could feel was the sinewy strength of those hands. They were so big that he was cradling her entire head, long fingers threading through her hair, massaging her scalp. And all the while his mouth and tongue were sucking her down into a deep spiral of the unknown.

When she stopped trying to pull his hands away she would never know. Nor would she be able to say when she moved her own hands and arms to wind their way up and over his shoulders.

She only knew that all reality had ceased to exist as they kissed and kissed with furious intensity. Their bodies were tight together and she pressed against the long, lean hardness of him. The thundering beating of their hearts was drowning out voices, concerns. She strained against him, on tiptoe to get even closer…could feel the unmistakable signs of his burgeoning arousal, and when she felt that her brain melted completely.

And then all of a sudden it was over, and he was stepping back from her. Angel made an awfully betraying move towards him, as if loath to let him go, her hands still outstretched from where they'd been wrapped like clinging vines around his shoulders. It was only then that she noticed her hands were held in his….and the awful suspicion arose. Had he had to forcibly take them down? Mortification flooded Angel even as she tried to assess the situation, gather her scattered nerves. Her heart still hammered. She was mute. Dizzy.

Leonidas Parnassus just looked at her, his face flushed…with anger? Or satisfaction that he'd proved himself right? Angel's mortification rose to a new level.

A discreet cough came from close by, and then a voice.

'Sir? If you could join your father inside now…*please*?'

Leonidas just looked at Angel, nothing given away on his face. It held a steely imperviousness that she would never have guessed the teasing man she'd met earlier to possess.

'I'll be right in.' Leonidas pitched his voice to reach the hovering staff member, but his eyes never left hers. He seemed to be utterly in control, apart from that betraying colour in his cheeks. She felt as if she was unravelling at the seams.

'I—' Angel began ineffectually.

He cut her off with an autocratic, 'Wait for me here. I'm not done with you yet.'

And with that he turned on his heel, and Angel watched him stride powerfully back into the thronged room, raking a hand through his hair as he did so. His back was huge and broad in the black of his tuxedo.

She couldn't believe what had just happened.

In shock she put a finger to her mouth, where her lips felt plump and bruised. Thoroughly kissed. In a fresh rush of embarrassment and disgust Angel could remember wantonly arching her body even closer to his...almost as if she'd wanted to climb into his skin. Not even in the most passionate moment of her relationship with Achilles had she felt that intensity of desire, every thought wiped clean from her mind. But then, she recalled bitterly, that had been part of the problem...

Angel felt raw and exposed, and painful memories were surging back, as if it wasn't awful enough to deal with what had just happened.

She heard a hush descend on the crowd in the salon, and searched for some means of escape. Finally, growing desperate, she spotted where some steps led down from the patio to the lower levels, and presumably back around to the kitchen. Hurrying down, she knew that she could forget about her job. The incident with the wine would have sealed her fate anyway; her disappearance with the guest of honour would have merely ensured it.

If her boss hadn't known the significance of who she was, he soon would, and she didn't want to be around to witness that.

Down in the kitchen she grabbed her things, and then crept out and headed down the drive, away from the glittering villa, not looking back once.

Leo stood and listened to his father's unashamedly emotional speech, Georgios Parnassus made no secret of the fact that he was ready to hand over the reins of power to Leo. The prospect of a shift in power had been evident in the room instantaneously. Again, Leo felt that welling of some ancient pride, that sense of right to be here. While he wasn't going to give the old man the satisfaction of capitulating so easily, he couldn't deny the sense of needing to stake his own claim to his birthright, the birthright that had been stolen from him.

His old man was no fool. No doubt he'd banked on exactly this by asking him to come to Greece, but Leo was not about to let him see that he might have won so soon.

Even while Leo was able to function and articulate his thoughts and intentions as the rapturous applause died away after his father's speech and the din of conversation rose again, his body still hummed with desire for the woman he'd left outside on the patio. He flicked a glance to the doors, once again open, but couldn't see her. Irritation prickled to think she might have moved. He'd told her to wait for him. He was trapped

now, though, by the usual sycophants, all vying
to get a slice of him.

He chafed to leave, to get back outside, finish
what they'd started, and that irked him. Here he
was at the potential forking of the road in his life,
a huge moment, and all he could think about was
a sexy waitress who'd had the temerity to blow hot
and cold and then hot again. Anger gripped him,
surprising him. He'd never encountered that
before. He'd had women play hard to get in an
effort to snag his interest and it never worked. He
didn't indulge in games. The women in his life
were experienced, mature…and knew the score.
No emotional entanglement and no game-playing.

But when *she* had looked at him as if he'd been
some callow youth trying to maul her…he'd seen
red. He'd never felt that singular desire before to
prove someone wrong, to imprint himself on a
woman. He'd never felt such a ruthless need to
kiss anyone like that…and then, when he'd felt
her initial struggle fade, when he'd felt her grow
hot and wanton in his arms, kissing him back
almost as if her life—

'Georgios couldn't have been more obvious—
so, are you ready to take the bait, Parnassus?'

Leo was so helplessly deep in his thoughts that
it took a second for his brain to function and come
back into the room. The fawning crowd surround-

ing him was gone. He blinked and saw that Aristotle Levakis, his father's business partner, was looking at him expectantly. Leo liked Ari Levakis; they'd worked closely together at the time of the merger, albeit with Leo based in New York. But, much to his chagrin now, he had to force himself to remember what Ari had just said.

He couldn't shake the building tension, wanting to get back out to *her*. What if she'd gone? He didn't even know her name. He forced himself to smile and joked, 'You think I'm going to discuss it with you and have any decision I make all over Athens by morning?'

Ari tutted good-naturedly. Leo tried to concentrate on their conversation even as he looked for glossy brown hair piled high, exposing a delicate jaw and neck.

He missed something Ari said then, and cursed himself. 'I'm sorry, what did you say?'

'That I was surprised to see *her* here. I saw you taking her outside—did you ask her to leave?' Ari was shaking his head. 'I'll admit she has some nerve...'

Leo went very still. *'Her?'*

'Angel Kassianides. Tito's eldest daughter. She was here working as a waitress... She spilt wine over Pia Kyriapoulos and you took her outside. I think everyone presumed that you were telling her where to go.' Ari looked around for a moment. 'And I haven't seen her since, so whatever you said worked.'

Leo had an instant reaction to hearing the Kassianides name mentioned. It was the name of their enemy; a name that represented *loss*, *pain*, *humiliation, and unbelievable heartache.* He frowned, trying to understand. 'Angel Kassianides… *She's* a Kassianides?'

Ari looked back and nodded, frowning when he saw Leo's face. 'You didn't know?'

Leo shook his head, his brain struggling to take in this information. Why would he know what Tito Kassianides' children looked like? They'd not dealt directly with the Kassianides family during the merger. The merger itself had been all that was needed to precipitate their downfall. It had been a clean and sterile revenge, but it felt curiously insufficient now, when he'd been faced by one of them here tonight. *When he'd kissed one of them.*

He felt acutely vulnerable; if Ari had recognised her, then who was to say that others hadn't? He remembered how he'd led her outside with one thought in mind: getting her alone so he could explore his attraction, with no clue as to her identity. He let anger dispel the unwelcome feeling of vulnerability. Had she been planning some sort of incident? What the hell had she been playing at with him? Seducing him with those huge blue eyes and then trying to pretend she didn't desire him? She'd been toying with him from that moment by the pool. Those widening eyes must have held recognition of who he was, not the mutual flash of attraction he'd believed it to be. The thought made bile rise. He hadn't felt so exposed…*ever*.

Had her father sent her, like some sort of pawn? Had the whole thing been an act? Leo's entire body stiffened in rejection of that thought. Just then he saw his own father approaching, with a delegation of other men. He had no time to process this now, and for the rest of the evening Leo would have to act and smile and pretend that he didn't want to rip off his bow tie, throw his jacket down and go and find Angel Kassianides and get her to answer some very pertinent questions.

A week later, New York

Leo stood at the huge window in his office that looked out over downtown Manhattan. The view was familiar, but he didn't see it. All he could see, and all he had seen every time he closed his eyes since Athens, was Angel Kassianides' angelic face, tipped up to his, eyelids fluttering closed, just before he'd kissed her. He laughed caustically to himself. *Angel*. Whoever had named her had named her well.

He wrenched his mind away from Angel and thought of Athens. Not that he'd admit it to anyone yet, and certainly not his father, but Athens had changed something fundamental inside him. New York was spread out below him and he felt nothing. It was as if even though he'd been born and brought up here it had never claimed him. It didn't resonate within him the way it once had. Now it was just a fast-living jumble of towering buildings.

He'd even rung his mistress that morning, after avoiding her all week, *which was not like him*, and broken it off. Her histrionics still rang in his ear. But he hadn't even felt a twinge of conscience. He'd felt relief.

Angel. It irritated him how easily she kept inserting herself into his consciousness. He hadn't been able to indulge in seeking her out and asking her just what the hell she'd been playing at in his father's villa due to a crisis erupting here in his head office. A crisis that looked set to continue for at least a few weeks, much to his irritation. Not that it was serving to take his mind off her. He wasn't used to women distracting his attention, and certainly not ones he hadn't even slept with.

Anger bubbled low within him. The feeling that he'd been made a fool of was a novel one, and not something he was prepared to allow for a moment longer. Angel Kassianides was playing with fire if she thought she could make a fool out of a Parnassus. Out of him. How dared she? After everything her family had done to his? On the very night of his public introduction to Athens society?

Her sheer audacity struck him again. Evidently the Kassianides family weren't content to let the past be the past. Did they want to rake up old enmity or worse, to fight to the death until they reined supreme again?

Leo frowned. Perhaps they had the support of some of the old Athens elite? Perhaps the threat was something to be concerned about…? And then, he chastised himself. Maybe it was all nothing. A pure coincidence that Angel had been there that night.

A small voice mocked: *was it a coincidence that out of all the people there, she was the one you noticed*? Leo's hands fisted in his pockets. He was not going to let her get away with this.

He turned around and picked up his phone and made a call. His conversation with the person on the other end was short and succinct. When he was finished he turned back to the view. Leo had just made a momentous announcement with the minimum of fuss: he was going to return to Athens and take over Parnassus Shipping. A tingling anticipation skated over his skin, made his blood hum.

The thought of facing Angel Kassianides again and forcing her to explain herself made the blood fizz and jump in Leo's veins. His jaw tightened as he fought the sudden surge of extreme impatience, a demand in his body that he act on his decision and go *right now*. He had things to do, his business in New York to sort out; a crisis at hand. He would bide his time and prepare, drive down this almost animalistic urge to leave. He assured himself that Angel Kassianides was not the catalyst behind his decision; but she was going to be one of his first ports of call.

CHAPTER TWO

A month later

ANGEL'S heart hammered painfully. She felt a cold sweat break out all over her body. For the second time in just weeks she was in the worst place in the world: the Parnassus villa. She felt sick when she remembered what had happened out on the terrace. She closed her eyes and breathed deep. She could not be thinking of that now. Of Leo Parnassus. Of how he'd made her feel just before she'd found out exactly who he was. Of how it had been so hard to forget him.

She opened her eyes again and tried to make out the rooms in the dim light. To her intense relief the place appeared to be empty, and she sent up silent thanks that for once the newspaper reports had been right. She'd read about Georgios Parnassus' ailing health, and how he was taking a rest on a recently acquired Greek island. She felt the reassuring bulk of the document in the inside pocket of her jacket. This was why she was here. She was doing the right thing.

Ever since it had been announced in the press just a few days ago that Leo Parnassus was taking over the reins of the Parnassus shipping fleet, and leaving New York to come back to Athens permanently, Angel had grown more skittish and her father more and more bitter and vitriolic, seeing any chance of redeeming himself diminish. A young, vibrant head of the Parnassus Corporation was a much bigger threat than the ailing father had been, despite their success.

Angel had returned home from her new job yesterday to find her father cackling drunkenly over a thick document. He'd spotted her creeping through the hall and called her into the drawing room. Reluctantly she'd obeyed, knowing better than to annoy him.

He'd gestured to the document. 'D'you know what this is?'

Angel had shaken her head. Of course she didn't know.

'This, dear daughter, is my ticket out of bankruptcy.' He'd waved the sheaf of pages. 'Do you realise what I'm holding here?'

Angel had shaken her head again, an awful sick feeling creeping up her spine.

Her father had slurred, 'What I'm holding is the

deepest, darkest secrets of the Parnassus family and their fate. *Georgios Parnassus' final will and testament.* I now know everything. About all their assets, exactly how much they're worth, and how he plans on distributing it all. I also know that his first wife killed herself. They must have hushed that up. Can you imagine what would happen if this was leaked to the right people? I can take them down with this.'

I can take them down with this. Nausea had risen from Angel's gut to think that after all these years, and after what the Parnassus family had been through, her father still wanted to fuel the feud. He was so blinded by bitterness that he couldn't see that doing something like this would make him and *his family* look even worse. Not to mention cause untold pain to the Parnassus family in revealing family secrets, if what he said about the suicide was true.

'How did you get it?'

Her father had waved a dismissive hand. 'Doesn't matter.'

Familiar cold disgust had made Angel bite out, 'You sent one of your goons to the villa to steal it.'

Her father's face had grown mottled, confirming what she'd said, or at least the fact that he had stolen it. She'd no idea how he had actually done it, but some slavishly loyal men still surrounded her father.

Her father had become belligerent, clearly done with her. 'What if I did? Now, get out of here. You make me sick every time I look at you and am reminded of your whore of a mother.'

Angel was so used to her father speaking to her like that she hadn't even flinched. He'd always blamed her for the fact that her glamorous Irish mother had walked out on them when Angel had been just two years old. She'd left the room, then waited for a while and gone back. Sure enough her father had passed out in his chair, one hand clutching the thick document, the other clutching an empty bottle of whisky to his chest. He'd been snoring loudly. It had been easy to slide the sheaf of pages out from his loosened fingers and creep back out.

Early that morning she'd gone straight to work, taking the will with her, knowing that her father would still be passed out cold. And then, late that evening, she'd taken the journey up to the Parnassus villa, but had panicked momentarily when faced with a security guard and the enormity of what she had to do. She'd blurted out something about being at the function some weeks before and leaving something valuable behind.

To her intense relief, after the unsmiling guard had consulted with someone, she'd been let in. To her further relief, when she'd reached the kitchens, she'd found no one and had crept up through the silent house, praying that she'd find the study. She'd leave the papers in a drawer and slip away again.

She was not going to let her father create more bad feeling between the families. That was the last thing they needed, the last thing Delphi needed. Every day now Stavros was begging Delphi to elope, but she was standing strong and refusing, determined not to ruin Stavros' prospects and be responsible for tearing his family apart.

The flaring up of their old feud with the most powerful family in Athens would make any prospect of marriage between them even more impossible. Angel heard her sister sobbing herself to sleep every night, and knew that a very real rift could break the young lovers apart for ever if something didn't happen soon. On top of everything else, Delphi had important law exams to think about.

The enormity of it all threatened to swamp Angel for a moment.

She emerged into the huge reception hall and stood for a moment, trying to calm her nerves, to stop her mind from spiralling into despair. Her breath was coming fast and shallow. She felt a prickling across the back of her neck and chastised herself. There was no one there. *Just get on with it*!

Seeing a half-open door across the expanse of

marbled floor, she held her breath and tiptoed across. Gingerly pushing the door open a little more fully, she breathed a sigh of relief once more when she saw that it was the study. Moonlight was the only illumination, and it cast the room in dark shadows.

Angel could make out a desk and went over, feeling for a drawer. Her fingers snagged a catch and she pulled it out, while reaching her hand into her pocket for the will at the same time. She'd just pulled it free and was about to place it into the drawer when the lights blazed on, with such suddenness and ferocity that Angel jumped back in fright.

Leonidas Parnassus stood in the doorway, arms folded, eyes so dark and forbidding that they effectively froze Angel from feeling anything but numb. And then he said quietly, but with ice dripping from his tone, 'Just what the hell do you think you're doing?'

Angel blinked in the intense light. She heard a roaring in her ears and had to fight against the very real need to faint. She couldn't faint. But she couldn't speak. Her brain and body were going into meltdown at being confronted with Leo Parnassus, standing just a few feet away, dressed in dark trousers and a plain light blue shirt, looking dark and intimidatingly gorgeous. Looking like the man who had invaded her dreams for the past seven weeks.

She opened her mouth, but nothing came out.

With a few quick strides Leo had crossed the room, moving so fast and with such lethal grace that Angel just watched in disbelief when he effortlessly whipped the will out of her white-knuckle grip.

'Well, Kassianides, let's see what you came for.'

Angel watched dumbly as he unfolded the document. She heard his indrawn breath when he registered what it was.

He looked at her, his dark gaze like black ice. 'My father's will? You came here to steal my father's will? Or just whatever you could get your dirty little hands on?'

Angel shook her head, registering that he'd called her Kassianides. It distracted her. 'You...you know who I am?'

His jaw tightened. Angel saw the movement and felt a flutter in her belly. He threw the will down on the table and reached out, taking her arm in a punishing grip. Angel bit back a cry at his touch, more of shock than pain.

He unceremoniously hauled her from behind the desk and led her over to a chair in the corner. He all but thrust her into it.

'I should have guessed after your last stunt that

you obviously don't have any qualms about trespassing where you're not welcome.'

He didn't answer her redundant question. Patently he now knew exactly who she was, and she realised that someone at the party must have told him after they'd seen him take her outside.

She knew it was probably futile, but she said it anyway. 'If I'd known for a second where I would be working that night I wouldn't have been here, I found out when it was too late.'

He all but sneered, towering over her now, arms crossed again over his broad chest. 'Please, give me some credit. You might be able to distract other people with that seductively innocent face, but after what I've just seen I know that you're rotten to your core. Your whole family are.'

Angel went to stand up on a fierce wave of anger. It was not fair to assume that she was like her ancestors, or her father, but before she could get a word out Leo had easily pushed her back down, not even using much force. Angel felt as weak as a rag doll, shaky all over. Once again the reality of his touch was more shocking than his action.

She clenched her fists and welcomed the rush of energy that anger brought. 'You have it all wrong. I'm not here to steal anything. If you must know—'

Leo slashed a hand through the air, silencing

her. Angel stopped abruptly. As much as she held no love for her father, she realised in that moment the futility of landing the blame at his door. Leo Parnassus would just laugh in her face. She'd quite literally been caught with her hand in the cookie jar, and could blame no one but herself.

She watched as he paced back and forth, his hands on his hips. The fingers were long and lean, and a sprinkling of dark hair dusted the backs of his hands. Suddenly an image of him hauling himself out of the pool that evening in one sleek movement caused heat to explode low in her pelvis.

In a moment of blind panic, feeling intensely vulnerable, Angel sprang up again and stood behind the high-backed chair. As if that could offer protection! Leo stopped and turned around to face her, surveying her coolly.

Angel asked huskily, 'What…what are you going to do? Are you going to call the police?'

He ignored her question and walked over to a sideboard, where he poured himself a measure of whisky. He downed the drink in one swallow, the strong bronzed column of his throat working, making Angel feel even more weak and trembly.

Leo's eyes snared hers again, and she saw something flame in the dark depths, revealing golden lights.

'Did your father send you here that night? Was it a recce for tonight? Or is this your own ingenuity?'

Angel's hands clenched on the back of the chair; she could feel her ponytail coming loose. 'I told you. The night of the party I had no idea where we were going. I worked for that catering company, they didn't tell us until we were on the way for security reasons.'

He all but laughed out loud. 'And once you and your father knew that Georgios was away, you took advantage of the opportunity. The only thing you didn't factor in was my return.'

'Th…there was nothing in the press.'

Leo glowered, and Angel quailed even more. Now she'd made it sound even worse. No way could she reveal that she'd been helplessly drawn to scanning the papers every day to read about his movements.

'I came a week early, hoping to surprise a few people. We're very aware—' his mouth tightened '—more so now we're in transition of power, that people will believe we're an easy target to take over.'

Angel had a nauseating realisation. 'You saw me arrive. The security guard checked with *you*…'

Leo indicated to Angel's right-hand side, and she looked over to see an ante-room off the study, the door through which he had appeared. In it, she could clearly make out a glowing wall of cameras, showing flickering black and white images. CCTV cameras. One of which looked directly over the main gate. He'd watched nearly every step of her progress. She felt sick when she thought of how she'd crept through the house. Her naivety mocked her. Of course she'd never have got near this place if he hadn't been here. She looked back.

Leo's face was so harsh that Angel felt a jolt of pure fear go through her. This man was a million miles from the seductive stranger she'd met that night.

'Your audacity is truly astonishing. Clearly you have the confidence born of your position in society, even if you don't hold that position any longer.'

Angel could have laughed if she'd had the wherewithal. Tito might have been wealthy once, but he was a despot and had controlled all their lives with a tight fist. It hadn't been audacity that had led her to that gate; it had been sheer fear and a desire to right a wrong.

'I wasn't coming to steal anything, I swear.'

Leo gestured back to the will sitting on the table and completely ignored her statement. 'What were you hoping to glean from it?' He laughed harshly. 'That's a stupid question. No doubt your father was hoping to use inside information on my father's estate to undermine him in some way. Or were you going to use the information to do a bit of honey-trapping, maybe? You'd have enough information to try and winkle out some more? Take advantage of the kiss we shared that night?'

Angel flushed hotly when she thought of that kiss, and then remembered her father's gloating talk last night. That was exactly how her father would think. Too late, she saw the hard, unforgiving look come into Leo's eyes, his jaw tense. Clearly he was misinterpreting her misplaced guilt.

Once again she knew that it would be futile to tell the truth. Leo Parnassus would be more likely to believe in Santa Claus than in her innocence, especially when the circumstantial evidence was so damning. All she knew was that she needed to get out of there. She was feeling increasingly hot and bothered under his intense and concentrated regard.

Tentatively she came from around the chair. She reassured herself that he was an urbane man of the world. An American. She had to be able to appeal to some rational part of him.

'Look. You have the will. I'm sorry for trespassing where I'm not welcome. I promise if you let me go that you'll never see or hear from me again.' Angel ignored the way her heart gave a funny little clench when she said that. She couldn't even begin to contemplate her father's reaction to what she'd done, and of course she couldn't promise that he wouldn't do something stupid again, but she kept her mouth shut.

Leo put down the glass silently on the table. Angel followed the movement warily. A strange charge came into the air between them and she found her eyes being helplessly drawn back to his. They were glowing with gold in their depths again, reminding her of how he'd looked at her just before he'd kissed her that night on the terrace. His eyes dropped then, insolently sweeping down her body, taking in her worn jeans, black top and jacket. Sneakers. And suddenly it was as if she was breaking out into little fires all over her skin.

Her heart started thumping. In a blind panic, to negate her reaction, she moved again, telling herself that he wouldn't stop her if she just walked out. After all, it wasn't as if she'd actually broken into the villa.

But just as she was about to pass him she felt her arm being gripped, and she was swung around so fast that she lost her balance and fell against him. All the breath seemed to leave her body.

In an instant he'd loosened her already unravelling hair, and it fell around her shoulders. His hand held her head, tilting her face up to him. His other arm was like a steel band around her back. Angel was afraid to move or breathe, because that would invite a contact that would scatter what remained of any coherent thought. As it was, she was barely clinging onto a shred of sanity.

'Do you know that you've actually done me a favour, Kassianides?'

Angel winced inwardly at his use of her surname, hating the fact that it bothered her.

'You've saved me a trip. Because I was going to confront you about why you'd come here that night. You couldn't possibly have believed you'd get away with it, could you?'

It was a rhetorical question. Angel said nothing, too scared of the burgeoning feelings and sensations running through her body. When Leo spoke again his chest rumbled against hers.

'I was also curious to know if perhaps I'd been too harsh in my first assessment as to why you'd been waitressing at our party. After all, just because you're Tito's daughter, perhaps it wasn't entirely fair to assume the worst.'

Angel couldn't believe it. She saw a glimmer of hope and started to nod her head. She opened her mouth, but he wasn't giving her an opportunity to speak. His voice became harder and harsher.

'But your actions here tonight have damned you completely. The minute you saw the opportunity you were back, and this time to steal something of real value that could be used in an effort to harm our family. That will has information about my own estate, so it's not just my father you've committed a crime against, it's me.'

Cold horror trickled through Angel. This was so much worse than she'd thought.

Leo continued, 'It's almost cute, how naive you were to think you could be so blatant. Do you really think if I hadn't been here that it would have been so easy to get access to this villa?'

Angel's fragile hopes died there and then. She tried to summon her strength and pull free, and regretted it immediately when it merely gave Leo more room to hold her even tighter against him. Her breasts were crushed against his chest. They were pressed together, torso to torso, hip to hip. His breath feathered near her mouth—when had his head moved so close?

She tried to pull back and his fingers tightened in her hair. She winced, even though he wasn't really hurting her. His mocking smile sliced through her defences.

'You can't be so naive as to believe you're getting away that easily, Kassianides, can you?'

Cold fear trickled through Angel. For a second she was distracted enough to ask, 'What do you mean?'

'There was another reason I was going to come for you.'

Angel shivered inwardly, he sounded so implacable. 'There was?'

He nodded, his face so close now that she felt as if she was drowning in the dark golden depths of his eyes. Her hands were between them, resting on his chest, where they'd gone in an instinctive move to steady herself. She could feel his heart beating steadily underneath them and it made her want to move her hips. She stayed rigid.

'You've kept me awake for weeks.' He grimaced. 'I tried to deny it, ignore it. But this desire wouldn't abate. I'm not in the habit of denying myself anything, or anyone I want. As much as I despise myself for feeling this…I want you, Angel.'

Angel's brain couldn't compute the significance of what he was saying, and certainly couldn't compute the tumult of emotions that had threatened to swamp her when he'd called her *Angel*. All those nights she'd woken sweating from torrid dreams…he'd been thinking of her too?

She tried to push back again, but Leo held her effortlessly. His head bent closer and Angel twisted hers away in desperation. He whispered near her ear with deadly silkiness, 'You came here that night to humiliate my family, and you tried to humiliate me. And you came here tonight to steal from us. You won't get away with it, Angel.

You can't expect to keep playing with fire and not get burnt.'

Angel turned her head back, seriously panicked now. She'd never stolen anything in her life! 'But I wasn't. I—'

But the rest of her words were silenced under the devastating crush of Leo's mouth to hers. He was ruthless, *he was angry*, and he plundered and took until Angel felt weak tears smart at the back of her eyes and her hands were fists trying to beat ineffectually against his rock-hard chest.

A weak moan of pleading came from deep in her throat. Finally Leo pulled away, and she felt his chest moving against hers with his harsh breaths. It should have disgusted her, *scared her*, made her recoil when she saw the heated look in his eyes, but it didn't.

It made her quiver deep down inside, somewhere very vulnerable. As if she'd been waiting for this. As if, despite everything, this somehow felt right. In that moment Leo's hand gentled on her head, his fingers massaged her skull, and the movement weakened her further. She couldn't cope with tenderness, gentleness. She felt a thumb move across her cheek, and only realised then that a tear must have crept out.

Leo smiled, but it was tight. 'The tears are a nice touch, Angel, but unnecessary—along with trying to pretend that you don't want me.'

He shifted slightly, so that Angel fell more into the cradle of his lap, and she gasped when she felt the hard evidence of his arousal against her belly. The shocking reality of it made moisture gather between her legs in a very earthy recognition of a mate. She couldn't believe she was having this reaction, and yet from the moment she'd seen him emerge from the pool…

She was caught by his eyes as if hypnotised. Everything melted away: who she was and why she was there.

When Leo bent his head again, this time he wasn't cruel and harsh. His touch was firm and seductive. His mouth settled over hers and caused a deep sigh to move through her.

With an expertise she dimly acknowledged Leo forced her mouth to open to him, touching his tongue to hers and causing a flash flood of liquid heat to her groin. Angel moved instinctively, barely aware of what she was doing, just sensing that she wanted…more.

Leo hauled her even closer, growling something in his throat as his mouth continued its dark magic on hers. Angel was vaguely aware that her hands had unfurled and had climbed up over those impossibly broad shoulders. She was now clinging to his neck, arching her body into his, fingers tangling in the surprisingly silky strands of his hair.

When Leo took his mouth from hers she gave a little mewl of despair. She opened heavy eyes to see him smile with sinful sexiness and her heart turned over. A lock of glossy black hair had fallen forward onto his forehead and Angel pushed it back with a trembling hand, barely aware of what she was doing, just following some deeply felt instinct.

Leo's hand settled at the waist of her jeans, and after a heart-stopping moment snaked under her top. The feel of him touching her bare skin made her pulse rocket skywards. His hand crept higher and higher, to where she could feel her breast grow tight and heavy, until after an excruciatingly slow moment he cupped the soft mound and pulled the cup of her bra down.

Angel bit her lip. She was seriously out of her depth, and she felt as if a part of her was standing apart and watching with mounting horror as she let him touch her so freely. But she was caught in the grip of something so powerful she couldn't move.

Leo moved his thumb back and forth over the tight puckered tip, and then with a brusque movement he thrust up her top to bare her breast to his gaze. To see him looking down at her breast made Angel feel faint with a rush of desire. And then, when he bent his head… Her mind was screaming at her to pull away…but she couldn't. When he flicked out a tongue and then sucked that peak into the hot, swirling cavern of his mouth Angel's head fell back. Her hands gripped his shoulders tightly.

She was fast being transported to a place of no return. The pleasure was so intense that she was afraid she'd burst. Leo brought a hand between her legs, forcing them apart to cup between her thighs, and she was lost completely. She'd never felt this out of control of her own body before.

He caressed her through her jeans, the material acting as a paltry barrier to his expert touch. He knew exactly where she ached, and all the while he suckled mercilessly on her breast. Angel cried out in desperation: for him to stop and for him never to stop. The sensation of her jeans and his hand moving remorselessly against her was excruciatingly exquisite.

Angel felt her body tensing. She'd lost any hope of regaining control by now. The world had ceased to exist. *This* was her reality.

With a husky whisper she entreated him, hardly knowing what she was looking for. '*Leo…*'

Everything went very still. But Angel hardly even noticed until, with sudden ruthlessness that almost bordered on cruelty, Leo stopped what he was doing and thrust her back from him with two hands on her shoulders.

For a long moment Angel stood in shock,

breathing swiftly as the earth righted itself again. Her heart thumped painfully and a light sweat had broken out all over her body. He rearranged her top and bra so she was covered again, with an abruptness that made Angel wince. The material chafed against her still sensitive nipple.

She just couldn't believe— Her thoughts ground to a halt when she realised her hands were glued to his chest, fingers curled and clinging to the material of his shirt. Hurriedly she dropped them as though burnt. Angel also realised then that her legs were incapable of holding her up, and she nearly collapsed in a humiliating heap at Leo's feet before he cursed and picked her up, bringing her back over to the chair and sitting her down.

Angel let her hair fall around her face. She couldn't find a word to articulate how awfully raw and exposed she felt. Leo had set out to humiliate her and it had taken a nanosecond before she'd turned into a groaning wanton in his arms. How he must be laughing at her. He'd accused her of stealing just seconds before he'd kissed her, and she'd all but lain down and given herself to him.

Her cheeks burned so hot they felt on fire. She could remember the way she'd said *Leo*, breathlessly, huskily, just as her whole body had been about to tip over the edge into an experience she'd never had, an experience that her jangling nerves craved to know even now. She'd thought she'd been in love with her boyfriend at college, and he hadn't even managed— She gulped. Yet here, with someone who clearly despised her... Mortification twisted her insides into hard knots.

'Angel—'

His voice was suddenly too close, and Angel jumped up in a reflexive surge of horrified anger at how she'd reacted. Too late she saw that Leo had been holding out a glass of what looked like brandy, and she could only watch dumbly as it was knocked out of his hand with the force of her jerky movement, spinning away to crash into the corner of the room, glass shattering, alcohol staining the parquet floor.

She looked at Leo in shock. 'I'm so—'

He cut her off, his face all sharp angles and forbidding lines. Jaw tense. 'You could have just refused, Angel. There was two of us involved in what happened just now, so don't try the outraged virgin act.'

If only he knew! His words fell like tiny cuts all over her skin. Angel quivered with a rush of contradicting and mixed emotions. Right then she was glad the glass had smashed, and yet she also wanted to rush to clean it up. She wanted to smack Leo across the face, when she'd never hit a soul in her life, but she also wanted to throw herself into his arms and beg him to kiss her again. Her body still tingled and burned.

She made a monumental struggle and tipped up her chin. 'I didn't see the glass. I'm sorry.'

His eyes flashed in response. In a bid to put space between them Angel went on jelly legs to where the glass had smashed and started to pick up the bigger pieces. She heard something inarticulate behind her, and gasped as she was pulled up, a hand under her arm.

'Leave it. I'll get someone to look after it.'

They were very close again, and all of Angel's recent humiliation rushed back. Something caught Leo's eye and he looked down at her hands, saying harshly, 'You're bleeding.'

Angel looked down stupidly. She hadn't felt a thing, but saw that her finger *was* bleeding from a nasty-looking gash. Leo expertly took the glass out of her hands and put it on the table behind them. Then, holding that hand carefully in his, he picked up the phone, dialled a number and bit out terse instructions in accentless Greek.

Angel would have been impressed if she'd been able to think clearly. All she could do was follow Leo when he led her from the room and up the main staircase, her hand held in front of him so she had to hurry to keep up with his much longer strides.

He brought her into a huge bathroom, switched

on the light, and rummaged around for something in a cupboard. Angel could see that it was a first aid kit, and blustered, 'Oh, no, don't. Let me—'

'Sit down and be quiet.'

Angel was forced to sit down on the closed toilet seat, and she watched incredulously as Leo knelt before her and inspected the cut. And then he brought her finger to his mouth and sucked it deeply.

Angel's breath stopped. She tried to pull back, but he was too strong. Finally he let her finger go and said tersely, while inspecting it again, 'I want to make sure there's no glass in it. It's a deep cut, but I don't think you need stitches.'

Thoroughly bemused, and feeling as if reality as she knew it had morphed out of all existence, Angel watched as Leo expertly and gently cleaned the cut and placed a tight plaster around the top of her finger.

Then, just as perfunctorily, he led the way back downstairs, this time into a drawing room adjacent to the other side of the hall. She saw someone scurrying out of the study with a dustpan and brush. Leo let go of her hand and Angel scooted over beside a couch, sitting gingerly on the edge because she didn't think she could stand.

Leo poured a measure of something dark and golden—*like his eyes*—into a glass and brought it over. His mouth was set in a grim line. Angel accepted it with both hands, while avoiding his eyes. She didn't drink much alcohol at all, but right now she welcomed the prospect of its numbing quality.

CHAPTER THREE

Leo watched Angel take the glass in both hands, a curiously child-like gesture that made something in his chest twist. He wanted to wring her pretty neck. But he also wanted to flatten her back against the couch and finish what they'd started in the study. He could still remember how it had felt to roll his tongue over her small tight nipple, the way she'd arched into him, and he had to use iron will right now to control the rush of response.

He had *not* meant to ravish Angel standing in the study like that. The impulse to kiss her had been born out of his inarticulate rage that she had such a visceral effect on him, especially when he knew exactly who and what she was. But the kiss had got out of control very quickly. He couldn't remember the last time he'd been so consumed, to the extent that he'd shut out every clamouring voice in his head. Until she'd said *Leo* with that husky catch, and her hips had jerked against his hand, and he'd emerged from what had felt like a trance.

He'd touched down in Athens barely three hours ago and was still reeling slightly at facing the reality that he'd willingly upended his life. Feeling acutely vulnerable *again,* Leo turned and strode back to the sideboard, to pour himself a drink and try and gather his scattered thoughts. They'd scattered as soon as he'd taken the call from the security guard and seen who was at the gate. For a disturbing second he'd almost believed he was imagining her.

And yet he couldn't deny that he'd felt a rush of pure sensual excitement at seeing Angel approaching the house. It had eclipsed the disappointment he'd felt that her effect on him hadn't grown less in the interim.

Her guilt had been obvious from the moment she'd gone straight to the kitchen entrance rather than come to the main door. And then, when he'd seen her creeping through the house like the little thief she was, something hard had solidified in his chest.

He hated to admit it but he *had* thought that perhaps he'd judged her too swiftly. Seeing the evidence of her avarice in front of his eyes tonight had made a fool of him *again*. She was no innocent. Hadn't years of witnessing hardened New York socialites in action taught him anything?

As he poured himself a drink now, and threw it back in one gulp, he told himself that his decision to come home and the speed with which it had been expedited had absolutely nothing to do with the woman sitting on the couch behind him. He knew exactly how he was going to deal with her and get her out of his system, so that he could get on with his new life here in Athens.

Angel sat on the couch, cradling her glass, and felt as if she was waiting to hear a sentence pronounced. Leo kept his broad back turned to her for long moments, and the tension in her body was beginning to ratchet up, despite the calming effects of the alcohol.

Eventually he turned around, and Angel almost breathed a sigh of relief. Leo's face was stark, unreadable. Not once had he cracked a smile, shown a glimmer of humanity…*apart from when he'd tended her cut*. Angel remembered the way he'd sucked her finger into his mouth and quivered deep in her belly.

She swallowed. She thought of how his lazy, easy American accent had made her assume he was just one of the guests at the villa that night… She'd never have suspected she'd ever hear the steel running underneath the velvet caress of that voice. But he was Leonidas Parnassus. Practically the uncrowned King of Athens. And she was his bitter enemy. Even more so now.

There was a final reckoning to be had between their families, and Angel was very afraid this was going to be it. She tried to force the fear down— after all, what else could happen to them now? She thought of Delphi then, and felt slightly sick.

Leo came over and took a seat on the couch opposite Angel. He sat back and crossed one ankle over one knee. He spread a hand out across the back of the seat, making the material of his shirt stretch enticingly across his chest. It was a dominantly masculine pose. Angel could feel her face heat up and willed it down.

'Why did you come here the night of the party?'

Angel couldn't believe it. Weariness tinged her voice. 'I already told you. I had no idea where we were headed. I couldn't have just walked out; I would have lost my job on the spot.'

'But you lost that job anyway,' he pointed out silkily.

Angel held in a gasp. How did he know that? Not that it would have taken a rocket scientist to deduce that her behaviour that night might result in that. Did he know that she'd been working as a chambermaid in the plush Grand Bretagne Hotel since then, and was doing regular double shifts? No doubt he'd love to know that she'd felt compelled to find jobs in areas where her name would require the minimum amount of investigation. She'd been conscious of Delphi still being in college, and had not wanted to draw any potential press attention by going for something more high-profile, only to get knocked back because of their name. Humiliation was becoming annoyingly familiar in this man's presence.

Leo took a sip of the drink he'd carried over. 'My picture was splashed all over the papers here the week I arrived. Your father has been scrabbling around like a rat in a sinking ship looking for someone to rescue him—and you expect me to believe that you saw me at the pool-side that night and had *no idea* who I was?'

She shook her head. She truly hadn't known, having instinctively shied away from reading anything about the Parnassus family and their triumphant return. It had been too close to the bone on so many different levels. Also, she'd been preoccupied with her sister's news.

Angel sat forward, hands clenched around the glass. From somewhere deep and protecting came a dart of anger at his high-handed arrogance, at how threatened he made her feel. 'Believe it or not, I had no idea. Aren't you satisfied that your family has done its level best to ruin mine?'

Leo let out a short, sharp laugh, making Angel flinch. 'I fail to see where the satisfaction comes when it's clear, based on the evidence tonight—which, I might add, is recorded on CCTV—that you are intent on re-igniting this feud. No doubt you have something to gain from it—most people would have moved on from the drama of the Parnassus family coming home.'

He sat forward then too, his eyes flashing sparks. Angel wanted to cower back, but held strong and cursed herself for provoking him. For a moment she'd forgotten all about why she was here in the first place. He scrambled her brain that much.

His tone was withering. 'And do you really want to play the game of apportioning blame?'

Angel felt something cold trickle down her spine when Leo's eyes turned dark and deadly.

'We have done nothing to affect your family directly. Your father's greed and ineptitude has seen to the demise of the Kassianides shipping fleet. All we had to do was merge with Levakis Enterprises, and that in itself highlighted the inherent weakness of your father's position.'

Angel swallowed. Everything he said was true. She couldn't really blame him or his father for having done anything concrete. Her father had done it all by himself.

'However,' Leo continued, sitting back like a lord surveying his subject, 'it leaves me with an interesting dilemma.'

Angel said nothing. She'd no doubt that Leo was about to enlighten her.

'While we've managed to get our due revenge in seeing the Kassianides fortune reduced to nothing, lower than even we were ourselves seventy years ago, I must admit that it feels somehow…empty. Since seeing the extent of your sheer boldness, I find myself desiring something of a more… tangible nature.'

Panic struck Angel. She felt as if an invisible noose was tightening around her neck. Desperation tinged her voice. 'I'd call going bankrupt pretty tangible.'

Leo leant forward again, utterly cold, utterly ruthless. 'The bankruptcy is for your father, not you. No, I'm talking about something as tangible as my great-uncle being accused of raping and then murdering a pregnant woman from one of the wealthiest families in Athens. As tangible as an entire family forced into exile from their homeland because of the threat of a criminal investigation they couldn't afford, and the possibility of my great-uncle facing the death penalty. Not to mention the scandal that would linger for years.'

'Stop,' begged Angel weakly. She knew the story and it always sickened her.

But he didn't. Leo just looked at her. 'Did you know that my great-uncle never got over the slur of being accused of that murder and eventually killed himself?'

Angel shook her head. She felt sick. This went far deeper than she'd ever imagined. 'I didn't know.'

'My great-uncle loved your great-aunt.' Leo's mouth twisted. 'More fool him. And because your family couldn't bear to see one of their own darlings slum it with a mere ship worker, they did their best to thwart the romance.'

'I know what happened,' Angel said quietly, her insides roiling.

Leo laughed harshly, 'Yes, everyone does now—thanks to a drunken old fool who couldn't live with the guilt any more, because *he'd* been the one who committed the crime and covered it up, had it paid for by your great-grandfather.'

Her own family had murdered one of their own and covered it up like cowards.

Angel forced herself to meet the censure in Leo's eyes even though she wanted to curl up with the shame. 'I'm not to blame for what they did.'

'Neither am I. Yet I paid for it all my life, I was born on another continent, into a community in exile, learning English as my first language when it should have been Greek. I saw my grandmother wither away a little more each year, knowing that she'd never return to her home.'

Angel wanted to beg him to stop, but the words wouldn't come out.

Leo wasn't finished. 'My father was so consumed it cost us our relationship. And it cost him his first wife. I grew up too fast and too young, aware of a terrible sense of injustice and a need to put things right. So while you were going to school, making friends, *living* your life here in your home, I was on the other side of the world, wondering how things might have been if my father and grandmother hadn't been forced out of their own country. Wondering if I might then have had a father who was present, not absent. Wondering what we had done to deserve this awful slur on our name. Do you have any idea what it's like to grow up being reminded that you don't belong somewhere every single day by your own family? Like you've no right to put down roots?'

Angel shook her head. She didn't think he'd appreciate hearing about how lonely she'd felt when her father had sent her to a remote and ultra-conservative catholic boarding school in the wilds of the west of Ireland. Somehow she didn't think that even the worst of her experiences there would come close to what Leo had described.

She felt hollow inside. 'Please, will you just tell me what it is you want or let me go?'

Leo sat forward, elbows on his knees, glass held casually between long fingers. Supremely at ease, as if he hadn't just related what he had.

'It's quite simple, really. I wanted you the moment I saw you, and I want you now.' His lip curled. 'Despite knowing who you are.'

Angel could feel her mouth opening and closing like an ineffectual fish. 'You don't. You can't.'

In a flooding of panic, Angel stood up. She carefully placed the glass down on a nearby table and hoped Leo wouldn't notice how badly her hand was trembling.

Leo stood too, and they faced each other across the expanse of a few feet.

'Sit down, Angel, we're not finished yet.'

Angel shook her head mutely, feeling the world start to constrict around her. Leo shrugged as if he didn't care. She tried desperately to block out the way he looked so intimidatingly huge opposite her.

'You're going to pay me back for everything you've done to me, and you will do it in my bed. As my mistress.'

Angel nearly burst out laughing, the need to release some of her pent-up panic almost emerging as hysteria. It faded, though, when she saw the look on his face. Her belly quivered.

'You're serious.'

'Of course I'm serious. I don't joke about things like this.'

A pulse beat in his jaw, making Angel's belly clench.

'Do you think I'm so naive as to assume your father is just going to roll over and take what's coming to him? I want you, and I want to keep you close, where I can see you—*away* from your father and his machinations. If that heat between us is anything to go by, I don't imagine it'll be unpleasant for either of us.'

Angel's belly quivered even more strongly and she felt slightly faint.

'You want to sleep with me?'

His mouth quirked dangerously. 'Among other things.'

'But…'

'But nothing. Everyone saw you and I at that party. I am not about to let you capitalise on that now that I'm back. Not to mention tonight's fiasco. You're a danger and a threat. You've had the audacity to come into my home twice, and now you'll pay for it.'

'But my father—' She stopped. *He will kill me*, Angel thought, with a mounting dread that had been born long, long ago.

Leo waved a hand in an abrupt gesture of insult.

'Your father I don't much care about. I'm hoping it'll cause him the maximum amount of humiliation when he sees his precious eldest daughter taken as mistress by his enemy. Everyone will know exactly why you are with me—warming my bed until I'm ready to move on, perhaps even settle down. Whatever you and he had planned, this will play out on my terms. And you can tell him that taking you as my mistress will afford him no honey-trap favours. Things still stand as they are. We certainly won't be bailing him out.'

Angel just looked at him, barely believing the direction their conversation had taken. She didn't see the point in revealing the reality of her dismal relationship with her father. He'd believe that as quickly as he'd believe her intentions had been honourable this evening.

So many things were impacting upon Angel at once, not least Leonidas Parnassus' cold and calculating words. She wanted to shout out that she didn't want him, that she didn't desire him, but her mouth wouldn't formulate the words. And in all honesty she was afraid of his reaction if she did say that. She was still smarting from what had happened in the study. She was far too vulnerable to him.

Feeling so cornered and impotent finally woke her from the stasis that had gripped her. He couldn't force her to do this. 'I'll gain nothing from this liaison because I won't do it. You couldn't *pay* me to be your mistress.'

Feeling panic escalate, right then Angel thought that even if he called the police and they charged her with trespass it had to be a better option than facing what he spoke of.

He looked at her steadily from under hooded lids. A flash of cynicism twisted his features for a moment. 'You're absolutely right. I wouldn't pay you. But you'll do it because you can't *not*. The desire between us is unfortunate, but tangible. You went up in flames in my arms just now, and you owe me after this stunt tonight.'

Derision laced his voice. 'Despite your words, as soon as you're in my bed you'll try and seduce as much out of me as you can. Playing hard to get might be a part of your repertoire, but I don't do games, Angel, so you're wasting your time.'

All Angel could feel was mortified heat enveloping her at remembering how she had come apart in his arms, literally. She made a jerky move towards the door, praying that he wouldn't touch her. She stopped when she felt safer. Leo hadn't made a move to stop her, but it didn't make her feel reassured. She turned back to face him and tipped up her chin.

'I won't be doing it because you're the last man on earth I'd willingly sleep with.'

She turned around, but just when she was about to put her hand on the doorknob she heard him drawl from behind her, 'Do you really think I'm about to let you walk out of here?'

Angel hated herself for not just turning the knob and walking out. She turned around again and tried to inject confidence into her voice. 'You can't stop me.'

Leo stood tall, legs spread, hands in pockets. He smiled, but it was feral.

'Yes, I can.'

Angel felt hysteria rising. She backed up to the door and felt for the knob in her hands behind her back, ready to run.

'What are you going to do? Kidnap me? Lock me away?'

Leo made a disparaging face. 'You've been watching too many Greek soap operas.'

He walked towards her then, and Angel gripped the doorknob even tighter, her whole body tense. He stopped a few feet away.

'Quite apart from the fact that I caught you in the act of stealing, and could call the police in for that alone, I will let it go—because I don't want our relationship to be mired in any more controversy than it's already likely to be when the press finds out.'

Angel blurted out, 'But we won't *have* a relationship, and I wasn't—' She stopped abruptly. Obviously Leo hadn't watched long enough to see her take the will *out* of her pocket. Which would mean that she'd have to explain how she'd got it. So either way it was still theft, albeit not by her. She was back to square one: damned by the actions of her father and her own impetuous desire to rectify matters.

Angel longed to toss her head and tell Leo she'd prefer to see the police, but she realised that she couldn't do that. It would cause the whole thing to explode in the press and she couldn't do that to Delphi. The noose was tightening.

Leo merely stood there and rocked back on his heels for a moment before saying, 'We do have a relationship, Angel, it started the evening of the party. And since then I've found out quite a wealth of information about you.'

Angel's hands were gripping the doorknob, shock still reverberating through her. 'What kind of information?'

'Well,' Leo started almost conversationally, 'I found out that you went to art college and studied jewellery design. And yet at no point since leaving college have you made any attempt to leave home, which can only point to a close relationship with your father.'

Angel bit back the explanation. It was her sister

she was close to, her sister she cared for, and her sister she had tried to create a stable environment for, because they'd never got it from their parents. After Damia's death, when Angel had come home from school in Ireland, she and Delphi had turned to each other for support.

A look of mock sympathy came over his harsh features. 'But since the collapse of Tito's business you've had to make ends meet by working for that catering company, and now working as a chamber maid for the Grand Bretagne. Tell me,' he said musingly, 'it must be hard, changing the sheets for people who were once your peers… I did wonder why someone as educated as you had resorted to menial work, but then I realised that you obviously want to avoid any unnecessary investigation into your disgraced name. No doubt you figured that you'd re-emerge on the social scene and find yourself a rich husband once the Kassianides name had lost some of its notoriety.'

Angel could feel the colour draining from her face at having it confirmed that he knew where she worked, and why she'd taken those jobs, albeit not quite for all the reasons he'd so cynically outlined. She thought of her dreams to set up a jewellery-making studio as soon as she had enough money. She thought of the aching disappointment she'd had to keep to herself every day that she hadn't yet been able to realise that dream.

'You have it all wrong. So wrong.'

He ignored her, and she could have had no warning for what he was to say next.

'Most interesting of all, perhaps, is that I also know that Stavros Eugenides and your sister are so-called sweethearts and want to marry, but his father won't let them.'

Angel's legs nearly gave way. 'How do you know that?'

He ignored her question. 'I will ask you this— is it important to you that your sister marries Stavros Eugenides?'

Angel felt sick inside. Her brain clicked into high gear and she shrugged minutely, trying not to let it show how hard her heart was thumping. She knew instinctively that if Leo guessed for a second just how important it was he'd go out of his way to not let it happen.

She tried to smile cynically, but it felt all wrong. 'They're young and in love. Personally I think it's too soon. But, yes, they want to marry.'

'I think you're lying, Angel. I think it's of the utmost importance to you and her that they get married. After all, why would you have gone to speak on their behalf with Dimitri Eugenides otherwise?'

Angel found herself starting to tremble violently. How on earth did he know this? Was he a magician?

'I—' But she got no further.

'I think that your sister is looking to get herself a rich husband just before you lose everything. If she can get engaged before the truly pathetic state of your father's affairs becomes public then she'll be safe. And you, by proxy, will be taken care of too.'

Angel shook her head, as much in negation of what he said than anything else.

Leo grimaced. 'In some ways I can't blame you. You're two poor little rich girls, just trying to survive. Unfortunately you don't seem to be aware that most of the world has to work to make a living to get through life.'

Angel shot into action and launched herself at Leo, her two hands aiming for his chest, but before she could hit him he'd caught them in the tight grip of his own hands.

Angel glared up, incensed to be feeling so weak and ineffectual. 'You have no right to say those things. You know nothing about us. *Nothing*—do you hear me?'

Leo looked down at Angel for a long moment, slightly stunned by the passion throbbing in her voice. He could see the twin thrusts of her high breasts against the thin material of her top. Immediately his body responded. Who was he kidding?

His body hadn't cooled down one bit since the study. And yet how dared she stand there and speak to him as if he'd just insulted her grievously?

With ruthless intent, he drew her in closer to his body. There were two twin flags of colour high in Angel's cheeks. Leo caught both her hands in one of his and caught her neck with his other hand, drawing her close. The tension spiked between them. He lowered his head, his mouth close to hers, and had to bite back a groan. She smelt so…so clean, and pure. With a hint of enticing musk. Just enough to make his body throb with need. This woman, she knew exactly what she was doing.

'I haven't finished with you, Angel.'

'Yes, we have finished. I'd like to go now.'

Leo could hear the tremor in her voice. Her breath tantalised him. He longed to crush her sweet, soft mouth under his again, but something made him hold back.

'We haven't finished because I'm not done telling you what I know. I can offer you something that despite your lofty protestations I don't think you'll be able to refuse.'

Angel finally jerked away from Leo's hands and stepped back, crossing her arms over her chest. The fact that he knew so much and could turn her upside down with just a touch was devastating. 'There's nothing you could say that I want to hear—'

'I can persuade Dimitri Eugenides to give his blessing to a wedding between his son and your sister.'

Angel's mouth was still open. She shut it again abruptly. She hated what she was giving away, but she had to ask, 'What…what do you mean?'

'Ah,' Leo mocked. 'Not so sure now that they're too young to marry?' A look of unmistakable triumph came into his eyes.

He was right, damn him, but for all the wrong reasons.

'Just tell me what you mean,' Angel bit out, vulnerability clawing through her.

'It's very simple. Dimitri wants to do business with me. The last time I was here he told me about the romance between his son and your sister, and thought he'd please me by telling me how much he disapproved, knowing of the history between the families. It had little significance for me at the time. Now, though, it has become…more significant. I can guarantee that as soon as it becomes apparent you're my mistress he'll be tripping over himself to make amends, terrified that I'll remember his less than favourable remarks. I can make it a condition of that business that he allows Stavros to marry your sister.'

Angel shook her head even as her heart fluttered with hope. 'He won't allow it, he hates our family.'

Leo waved aside her concern and said arrogantly, 'He'll do whatever I ask, believe me. The man is desperate to enlist my favour.'

Without really thinking, Angel found a chair nearby and sank into it. Her brain was buzzing. With a click of his fingers Leo had honed in on the one thing that Angel wanted most in the world—to be able to make things right for Delphi. She looked up at Leo, standing there like a marauding warrior, legs planted wide apart.

She didn't care what he thought; she just knew she had to do whatever it took. She stood up again. 'I presume your condition for doing this is to make me agree to become your mistress?'

Leo's mouth thinned, and a hint of anger came into his eyes. 'Don't try and dress this up into you being the unfortunate victim. We both want each other, Angel, you just seem determined to deny it.'

'But essentially you won't help Stavros and Delphi unless I agree to go to you?'

Leo shrugged insouciantly. 'Let's just say that then I would care even less what happens to them than I do right now. Why would I put myself out like that unless I was getting something in return?'

'Me,' Angel said flatly, but with an awful telltale quiver of physical response in her belly. She couldn't even tell herself that she was immune to or disgusted by Leo's offer, and she hated herself for it. Her conscience pricked her. *How* could she walk away from this opportunity for her sister and Stavros to be happy, no matter how it was coming about?

Angel's mind became very clear as she saw all her options dwindle away. Delphi was the best part of three months pregnant, and wouldn't want the ignominy of everyone knowing that on her wedding day.

'If I agree to this, I have a condition of my own.'

Leo's eyes flashed a warning. 'Go on.'

'I want Delphi and Stavros to be married as soon as it can be arranged.'

That look of cynicism that Angel was beginning to recognise all too easily crossed Leo's face again.

'Don't think that by having them marry as soon as possible it'll indicate the end of our affair, Angel. I won't let you go until I'm good and ready.'

Angel's belly quivered again. How would he react when he discovered she was a virgin? He didn't strike her as the kind of man to entertain novices in his bed.

Leo was looking at her assessingly. 'But I don't see why I can't fulfil that request. Not when you're mine from this moment on.'

Angel felt the colour drain from her face.

Leo didn't like the way Angel had just paled so visibly. He strode over to where she stood and snaked out a quick hand to caress the back of her neck again. He felt the silken fall of her hair over his skin, and it made his voice rough with suppressed desire. 'There's no time like the present. I'll have my car take you home, so you can pack some things and be brought straight back here to me.'

Just like that.

CHAPTER FOUR

LESS than three hours later, Angel stood in the hall of her own house, a suitcase at her feet. When she'd finally left the Parnassus villa she'd been aghast to see that dawn had been breaking, it had made her feel acutely disorientated. By some miracle her father wasn't at home; Angel's more and more harried looking stepmother informed her that her father had left the previous evening for London, to try and beg a loan from his cousins. Angel had been dreading the inevitable showdown with him, for undoubtedly he'd know that she'd taken the will.

She'd gone into her sister's room and woken her up and told her what was happening, while omitting the real reason why Leo was asking her to move in with him. Delphi had been understandably concerned. 'But, Angel, they *hate* us. They must do. What do you mean, you just happened to meet him and he swept you off your feet? It's all so fast and you never said anything…'

Angel hated lying to her sister. She'd smiled tightly and explained how they'd met at the party, and how she hadn't wanted to say anything in case their father found out. 'Delph, I didn't want you to be worried. I wasn't sure what to expect myself, wasn't even sure if he'd come back to Athens. But he has...' Here Angel had flushed hotly, remembering his kiss in the study. 'And he wants me to move in...I know it all seems weird and too fast and unlikely...but just trust me, please? I know what I'm doing.'

Delphi had completely misread Angel's acute embarrassment as being infatuation, but even so it had only been after more grilling that she'd finally seemed satisfied with Angel's answers.

When Angel had taken a deep breath and told Delphi about Leo's link to Stavros' father, and what he'd promised to do for them, and seen her ecstatic reaction, she'd known then that she had no choice but to follow her fate.

As if she'd had a choice anyway. Leo could still call the police and accuse her of stealing. No court in the world would believe her over him, with the evidence he had. But, apart from that, she couldn't jeopardise Delphi and Stavros' happiness now—their bid for independence and the future security of their baby.

For the first time Delphi had sounded grown up.

'Angel, you don't have to be responsible for everything, you know. Just doing this for us is enough. I'll be fine here, I promise. It's time you got to live your own life.'

Angel might have laughed at that if she hadn't known that she would be in danger of it turning to tears. She wouldn't be free to live her life now until Leo had decided he'd had enough of her. Her only hope was that her woeful inexperience would be enough of a turn-off for him that he would be content to use her like some kind of trophy mistress until he deemed she'd paid her dues.

But why, when she thought of that, did her womb contract with what felt like disappointment? Angel quashed that thought down ruthlessly. Her mind was just playing tricks. She'd just made a call to the hotel where she'd worked and resigned her job; there was nothing left to do. She took a deep breath and picked up her small case. It was time to go.

'Won't your father be here at the villa too?'

Leo had led Angel into a palatial bedroom, the sheer understated luxury of which had made her eyes goggle. Her father's taste had always been seriously lacking, he being the kind of person who believed trappings like gold taps were the sign of a rich man.

Leo was in the act of showing Angel where a door connected with his room, and she'd blurted out the question as much to disguise her panic as anything else. Now he turned and leaned nonchalantly against the doorjamb.

In the few hours since she'd left the villa and returned, she was disgusted to see that Leo looked as if he'd had a full night's sleep and was as rested and vibrant as anyone had a right to be. She felt sticky all over, with gritty eyes, and still dazed from everything that had happened.

The rumble of his voice brought her back. 'My father is staying on the island indefinitely. His doctors have advised no stress, and Athens means stress because he's incapable of staying away from work. Even now.'

Angel winced at the bitter edge to Leo's voice, and was reminded uncomfortably of what he'd revealed about their relationship. Irrational guilt assailed her. She could say nothing to that; any murmur of sympathy or empathy would be shot down in an instant. Anyway, Leo was ignoring her, revealing another room.

Angel had seen the *en-suite* bathroom, as big as her bedroom at home, and now Leo was pointing to an empty walk-in wardrobe. She came closer and looked in warily.

Leo sent a cursory look up and down her body

and Angel fought not to cringe. She was still in the same clothes.

'I'll have a stylist come to consult with you tomorrow, and sort out a full wardrobe. We can't have you looking anything less than a bought woman from now on, can we?'

Angel caught a flash of the huge bed she'd been ignoring in her peripheral vision and it scared her silly, making her say flippantly, 'Knock yourself out. Fill that wardrobe and I'll be only too happy to act out the part.'

He pushed himself off the door, coming close enough to have Angel's panic and pulse zoom skywards. He smiled lazily. Cynically.

'I don't think it'll take too much acting. Your skittishness is intriguing me. I would have expected you to be ecstatic that I've chosen you as my mistress. You forget that I come from New York…the natural habitat of the mercenary, gold-digging socialite. Your black soul won't surprise me, really.'

Angel searched for words, but to her chagrin couldn't get them out in time. To her consternation, Leo merely looked at his watch then, and said crisply, 'I have to go to the office. Why don't you get some rest? You look tired.'

And then he was gone, and she was alone. Angel walked into the bathroom and looked at herself in the mirror. She didn't just look tired. She looked shell-shocked. Feeling incredibly weary, and more than a little numb, she stripped off and stood under a steaming hot shower for a long time.

And then she got out, dried her hair, shut the curtains, crawled into the softest bed she'd ever felt, and fell into a deep dreamless sleep.

The first thing Angel knew was a gentle rocking. And then a voice. A deep, soulful voice that she found herself instinctively turning to. She smiled. The rocking became more forceful, and so did the voice.

'*Angel*.'

She wasn't dreaming. In an instant she was awake. Wide awake. Looking up with big eyes at Leonidas Parnassus, who was far too close to her, sitting on the bed, his face inscrutable. It all rushed back. She wasn't in her own bed; she was in his home and had agreed to become his mistress.

Angel grabbed for the sheet and pulled it up, even though she was dressed in pants and a vest. She scrabbled back as far as she could go, away from him. She felt exposed at having been caught sleeping. How long had he been there?

Leo stood up from the bed and Angel asked huskily, 'What time is it?'

He consulted his watch. 'It's 8:00 p.m.'

Angel sat up in shock, still holding the sheet. 'I've been asleep *all day*?'

Leo nodded and went over to pull the curtains back, so Angel could see the sun starting to set in the sky. She felt completely disorientated—jet-lagged, almost. Leo started to walk out of the room, barely glancing at Angel now. 'Dinner will be served in twenty minutes. I'll wait for you downstairs.'

While he waited for Angel, Leo stood at the huge French windows of the less formal dining room. The doors were opened out onto the terrace—the same terrace he'd brought Angel out to on the night of the party. He could scarcely fathom that he'd been in Athens for barely twenty-four hours and already had Angel in his home. Yet bizarrely it felt right.

Just now, when he'd woken her, he'd seen something that had reminded him of that first evening they'd met. For a moment before she'd woken she'd almost turned to him, with a soft smile around her mouth, and that enticing beauty spot at the corner of her lip had made him want to bend down and kiss it. Made him want to do so much more. When she'd opened her eyes, though, he'd noticed slight shadows still lingering.

Her hair had been sleep-mussed, tangled over one bare shoulder, where the strap of her vest had fallen down. She'd looked incredibly sexy, yet unbelievably vulnerable, and he had felt a niggle of unease at how quickly things had progressed from him finding her creeping through the villa. He'd pushed the unease aside. Even those three hours waiting for her to return had been torturous. He'd actually been nervous that she wouldn't return. That, despite everything he had on her, she would defy him. Leo noticed his hands had gone into fists now, just thinking about it. He forced them to uncurl.

He thought of how she'd looked when she'd returned, with shadows like bruises under her eyes...

She'd come into his family home to steal from them.

With more effort than he liked to admit, Leo pushed down the concern. A tight coil of desire held him in its grip. Tonight he'd have her, and he'd no doubt that within a very short space of time she'd prove to be as dismayingly predictable as every other woman he'd ever met, ultimately using emotion arising from intimacy, thinking that she could manipulate him.

He heard a noise at the door and turned around slowly. It was time for Angel to face the consequences of her actions.

* * *

Angel's skin prickled when she was shown into a dining room by a smiling housekeeper and saw Leo standing with his back to her. The windows were open and the curtains fluttered on the breeze. She had no idea how to act in this situation. No idea what was expected of her. She felt acutely lonely all of a sudden.

Leo turned around slowly, and the impact on her senses was nothing short of cataclysmic. She'd not really noticed what he was wearing in her room; she'd been too shocked and groggy. But now she saw that he was dressed in a pair of lovingly worn and faded jeans, which clung to him like a second skin. The material stretched over powerful thighs and long, long legs.

A black polo shirt made the brown of his eyes seem even darker, his skin seem even more olive. His shoulders were almost too broad for the material, and huge biceps bulged from beneath the short sleeves.

'Come and see the view, Angel.'

I'm already looking at it, she felt like blurting out slightly hysterically.

Knowing she was in a situation she couldn't get out of, her fate sealed by her own stupidly impetuous actions and her wanting to make everything all right for Delphi, Angel walked over to Leo, very self-conscious in her plain black shift dress. Hair pulled back. She coloured when she saw his gaze drop. She'd viewed him on Google him in a moment of weakness and seen exactly the kind of woman he went for: invariably tall, blonde, soignée. *Experienced.* A million miles from herself.

'Very demure,' he murmured when she came close.

'If I'd known casual was okay I would have worn jeans too,' she said stiffly, her gaze resolutely fixed on the view of Athens spread out below them. Not even that spectacular vista could distract her from the man beside her.

'I like to be casual at home, Angel, so here you can wear what you want…even go naked if you wish,' he finished softly.

Angel coloured even more at his mocking tone, wondering what on earth he saw in her. 'I don't think so.'

'Pity.'

She heard him pour some wine into a glass, and then he was offering it to her. She took it—anything to try and give her some courage.

'What do you think of the view—it's amazing, no?'

Angel snuck a quick look up; Leo was staring out, his profile to her, showing that he had a slight bump in his nose, and she could see the faint raised line of the scar over his lip. Hurriedly she looked back, afraid to be caught staring.

'Yes, it's truly beautiful.' Amidst everything, she thought of something else, and looked at her watch to check the time. 'Actually, any minute now…yes, there. Look—' Angel lifted her hand to point to where the evening lights were coming on to illuminate the Acropolis, far below in the distance.

She heard Leo's intake of breath and couldn't look at him, for some reason afraid of what she might see. It was always a magical sight, and one that took her breath away too. Was it having the same effect on him? She felt a lurch to think that she'd grown up seeing it as an everyday occurrence but he hadn't.

'I've seen the lights before, but never the moment when they come on like that.'

Angel murmured something inarticulate feeling unaccountably guilty. She turned with more than a little relief when the housekeeper bustled in with their food, and Leo turned too, indicating for her to precede him to the table.

Leo watched Angel walk in front of him, took in the glossy hair tied back in a low, careless bun, the long, elegant neck. And looked down to where her bare legs were slender, yet shapely enough to make his heart kick and his pulse throb.

Her palpable air of nervousness had caught him

unawares as she'd stood beside him. He had to question why she was feigning it *now,* when they both knew where they stood. She'd been nervous before, in the study, but that had no doubt been because she'd no idea how he'd react to catching her red-handed.

He'd certainly not been prepared to have her point out a sight she must have seen a thousand times before, which must be wholly unremarkable to her but had taken his breath away, seeing it for the first time. In any other instance he would have considered it a sweetly considerate gesture.

She wasn't acting the way he'd imagined she'd act in this situation. He'd expected a certain initial belligerence, or even defiance at having been caught and manipulated so spectacularly. Or he'd imagined that she'd want to make the most of the situation and take advantage of becoming his mistress. Leo had yet to meet a woman who didn't see the advantage in becoming his mistress, so for her to be feigning this nervous skittishness was going to get her nowhere fast.

They sat down. Leo looked at Angel darkly, but she was avoiding his eyes. Straightening her cutlery, her napkin. She was up to something. She had to be. Trying to disarm him for some reason. He reminded himself that she'd been home earlier, and of course she must have taken advice from her father. Leo cursed himself. The fact that he didn't trust Angel was not in question, so why was he trying to decipher her behaviour? The only behaviour that concerned him was her good behaviour as his mistress, on his arm and in his bed. Anything above and beyond that was of no interest to him.

Angel was doing her best to eat the deliciously prepared dinner, but it tasted like sawdust in her mouth. All she could see, all she could think about, was the man eating his dinner at the head of the table to her left. Her eyes kept being drawn to his hands, how powerful they looked. The tension mounted and mounted, especially when she thought of those hands in other places. On her.

Leo, however, seemed happy to concentrate on his food. Angel had countless questions bubbling on her lips: did he expect to sleep with her tonight? What would he do when he discovered how inexperienced she was? Would he reject her outright, as Achilles had? And why did that thought hurt so much? Why was she so consumed with him when he was all but blackmailing her into his bed?

Angel had never felt more confused, and very, very vulnerable. The silence, she was sure, was Leo's way of unsettling her, reminding her she was here for just one purpose. A purpose she was woefully ill prepared for. He wasn't even attempting small talk. When she felt something brush against her bare legs under the table she let out a startled cry, and dropped her knife to the floor with a clatter.

Just then the housekeeper came back in—Leo had introduced her to Angel earlier as Calista—and Angel saw that it had just been a cat. Her cat. After profuse apologies, and her knife being replaced, they were alone in the room again.

Leo put down his knife and fork and Angel jumped minutely.

'Why so tense, Angel?'

She looked warily at Leo. His eyes were dark, like mysterious pools. He was all hard angles and shadows. A dark line shadowed his jaw after a day's growth.

'I…' She couldn't articulate a word. Something dense was in the air around them all of a sudden, something tangible and electric. *Was this desire?*

'No appetite?' he asked then innocuously, with a raised brow.

Angel just shook her head and watched, dry-mouthed, as his gaze fixated on her mouth. It tingled. God, why couldn't she be immune to him and stand up in disgust and tell him if he touched her she'd call the police? Because then he'd probably call the police himself, send her away, and Delphi and Stavros would be back to square one. Worse, with the ensuing media storm.

However, those very good reasons aside, with the heavy weight of inevitability, the real reason sank into her head: she wanted him to touch her. The truth was shocking when she acknowledged it. Despite everything, she *wanted* him to touch her. Had done from the moment she'd seen him emerge from the pool…and from the moment he'd kissed her on the terrace. Since that night she'd had dreams, when she'd woken in sweaty tangled sheets, aching… And it killed her to admit it. Especially when she'd all but written sex off after her first experience.

Her hormones had turned traitor and were in league with this man.

Leo suddenly pushed his plate away and stood up, towering over her. His eyes glittered with a dark promise. A muscle popped in his jaw. 'I find that my appetite for food has gone, too.'

There was something rough in his voice that resonated deep within her. When he held out a hand, Angel hesitated for a second before putting her hand in his. She told herself this was just part of the agreement. She was securing Delphi's freedom and happiness. He wasn't throwing her to the police with accusations of theft. All she had to do…all she had to do… She stumbled as Leo led her from the room. They encountered Calista on the way, and Leo explained in rapid Greek that they were both tired and going to bed.

Angel's cheeks burned as Leo led her up the stairs. She was mortified. She tried to tug her hand back, panic making her voice high. 'She's going to know exactly what we're doing.'

Leo's voice was hard. 'You're my mistress. I should hope so. And if the gossip here is anything like in New York, it'll already be halfway round Athens by morning that I have taken Angel Kassianides into my bed.'

CHAPTER FIVE

His stark words rendered Angel mute. She felt she had no choice as Leo led her into his bedroom. She chastised herself; there was always a choice. But her choice to retain her dignity and walk away would have an effect on the person closest to her.

And she found as Leo kicked the door shut with one foot and led Angel further in, close to his massive bed, that the desire to walk away was disturbingly elusive. She hated to admit it to herself, but was she using Delphi in some way to justify this?

Disgusted with herself, because that was a very real possibility, Angel wrenched her hand free from Leo's. The very pertinent fact of her virginity had also been easy to push down to somewhere she didn't want to explore. But now it was rising again. How could it not, when it was about to become an issue?

Angel backed a few feet away from Leo and stood tall. 'I'm not going to just fall into your bed like some concubine.'

His mouth tightened. 'No, there's a more modern word: mistress. You'll fall into my bed like the mistress you are. I'm sure you've done it for countless others, Angel, no need to be shy.' He smiled, and it was cruelly mocking. 'It's lucky I caught you between lovers.'

'How…?' Angel asked shakily, the wind taken out of her sails. 'How do you know I don't have a lover?'

Leo walked over to where she stood. 'Because I've had you followed since I left Athens and your every move reported back to me. So you see, Angel—' here Leo reached out and tucked some wayward hair behind her ear '—I know that you must be dying to get a taste of the life you've undoubtedly been missing, thanks to your father's excessive greed.'

He lifted up her hands, which were dry and a little rough from all the cleaning she'd been doing. Each time she'd had to scrub a toilet she'd imagined the day when she'd be polishing the white gold of one of her jewellery designs.

With no clue as to what was in her head, Leo brought her hands up to his mouth and kissed them one by one, making Angel's heart speed up even as delayed shock made her useless. *He'd had her followed?*

'You can't deny that you aren't craving the easy life again, Angel, and I can provide that for you.'

Bitterness that he had so little idea of who she really was made Angel say, 'Just temporarily, though.' She knew saying that would most likely give him the impression that she was greedy, and she hated that she cared.

He quirked a brow and dropped her hands, but kept hold of them. 'It's up to you, Angel. It depends on how much you please me in bed…'

Bed. Panic exploded in her gut. He thought she was experienced, really experienced. And, to give him his due, most of the girls in her peer group were. She and Delphi, they were a breed apart—always had been, thanks to Tito's excessively controlling nature, and the fact that he'd had Angel all but locked away in a remote school for most of her teenage years. It was why their sister Damia had rebelled and come to such a tragic end.

'Leo, I don't think you understand—'

He came even closer and snaked a hand around her neck, drawing her mouth up to meet his. 'There's nothing to understand, Angel except *this*.'

Leo tipped her chin up, and before she could react his mouth was on hers for the second time in just twenty-four hours. So much had happened in so little time that Angel's head reeled, but it was all being washed away as Leo's mouth moved seductively against hers, eliciting a response that she couldn't deny.

With a muted groan of despair at her own helpless reaction, Angel let her hands find their way to Leo's chest, where they clung to his shirt. She had to hang on or she'd fall down in a heap. She could not understand how this man had such an instantaneous effect on her, but he did.

His tongue sought hers and made her insides melt into a pool of lust, just by stroking it. Their mouths clung. Angel remembered the study and her awfully wanton response, how he'd left her so unsatisfied. But she didn't have time now to feel humiliated; all she could feel was that new-found ache, growing again.

Leo's hands were on the back of her dress; the zip was being drawn down. Angel pulled away and looked up. Her chest rose and fell rapidly, and her heart was thumping so hard she felt faint. Her mouth felt bruised and swollen. She could only stand there as she felt a cool breeze whistle over her skin as the zip descended. All the while Leo was holding her gaze and not letting her look away.

When the zip was all the way down, to just above her buttocks, Leo pulled Angel in close again and smoothed his hands up and down her naked back. Electric shocks of sensation made her shudder; the tips of her breasts tingled. She felt him undo the clasp of her bra. Things were moving quickly…too quickly.

Jerkily Angel pulled away from Leo's caressing, distracting hands. The dress gaped forward slightly, and she put up her hands to stop it falling. She knew now that she'd blocked out the reality of what it would mean to do this.

But just when she went to open her mouth to say something Leo started pulling off his own clothes. Her eyes grew huge, and between her legs she throbbed when he stood before her naked, like a proud warrior. His broad, superbly muscled chest and shoulders had been awe-inspiring when she'd seen them, but when her gaze dropped Angel's breath stopped altogether.

A taut, flat belly led down to a thatch of dark hair from which sprang a truly intimidating erection. Angel had only ever seen one man in this state, and that would never have prepared her for *this*. Leo stood proud, legs apart, thighs heavily muscled, cradling his impressive masculinity.

There was a blur of movement and Angel felt her dress being pulled away and down her arms. Suddenly it lay in a pool of black at her feet. She gave a squeal of protest but Leo was remorseless, and somehow, with an economy and efficiency of movement that took her breath away, she stood before him in just her panties. Her hair fell about her shoulders. She put an arm across her breasts and a hand down to cover between her legs.

Leo chuckled darkly, 'There's really no need to act the innocent…'

'But I'm not—'

'Enough talking,' he growled, and stopped her words with his mouth again, his naked body coming into hot and immediate contact with hers. Angel's brain went into meltdown. He took her arm away from her breasts, and Angel's brain nearly short-circuited when she came into contact with that turgid erection.

Despite the wild excitement that flared through her body she wasn't ready for this. She'd never be ready for this. She'd had some dim and distant hope that perhaps she could pretend, that her virginity might not be glaringly obvious, but that hope laughed in her face now.

Leo was backing her towards the bed, pushing her down. Things were moving too fast. She had to stop him, even though knowing that he was naked and feeling his smooth olive skin next to hers was turning her thoughts to mush.

Angel couldn't bear for them to get to the point she'd reached before with Achilles and have Leo look at her with the same awful dawning horror on his face when he found out she was a virgin. Angel could remember the excruciating pain, the awful humiliation when Achilles hadn't been able to penetrate her. He'd shouted at her, told her she was frigid, that no one would want to sleep with her because she was a virgin.

And even though Angel felt in her body instinctively that *this* was different, that the same outcome wasn't assured, her brain was warning her of the pain and humiliation to come. And she knew that, however bad it had been with Achilles, to face the same from Leo would wound her so much more deeply, and that knowledge alone was enough for her to call a halt.

With a mammoth move, Angel pushed at Leo's chest. One of his hands was travelling up her leg, and already she could feel herself weakening, moistening. Her body wasn't hers any more.

She shoved again, and knocked his hand away with enough violence to make it sound like a slap, 'No!' The sound echoed in the room.

Leo's movements stilled over her.

She looked up at him and bit her lip. All she could see were the strong planes of his face. He too was breathing harshly.

'I…I have to tell you something.'

After a long moment Leo pulled back and reached over to put on a lamp beside the bed; it cast out a warm pool of low light. Abruptly he plucked his jeans off the floor and pulled them on roughly, standing up.

Angel felt very exposed and sat up, grabbing the sheet and pulling it around her.

Leo stood with hands on his hips, jeans undone. She could see the bulge of his arousal. He oozed such potent virility in that moment that Angel knew she was right to stop this now; she was no match for him. He needed a woman with experience, a woman to equal him, a woman like the women she'd seen on the internet. She felt sick.

'Well, Angel? This had better be good.'

Angel would have stood, but the sheet was tucked into the bed so she sat awkwardly, holding it against her. She looked down for a moment, gathering her courage, and felt the welcome curtain of her hair around her face.

She looked up finally, and spoke at the same time as Leo.

'Angel—'

'I'm a virgin.'

They both stopped. Leo looked at her. A strange stillness seemed to come into his body, and the air grew thick with atmosphere around them.

'What did you say?'

Angel gulped. 'I said that I'm a virgin.'

Leo shook his head. 'No, it's impossible.'

Angel felt the cold trickle of humiliation come into her body. This was going to be so much worse than she'd envisaged. On an impulse to cover up properly she scooted quickly from the bed and plucked her dress off the floor, stepping into it and pulling it up over her chest, clutching it there with her hands.

She looked at Leo and fought to stay standing in the face of his obvious disbelief. 'I'm afraid it is possible. I'm not what you…' She bit her lip. 'I've never been anyone's mistress.'

Leo's hand came out in a slashing movement; anger throbbed in his voice. 'You're lying. This is some game you're playing. I've told you, Angel, I don't play games.'

'Neither do I,' she said miserably. 'And believe what you want, Leo, but I don't think it would take long to prove you wrong.'

Leo just stared at her, his hands bunched into fists on his hips. It was as if he was trying to see inside her very soul.

Angel couldn't take the intensity of his regard. She looked down and stupidly felt she had to apologise. She quashed the impulse. 'We didn't… there hasn't exactly been the opportunity to discuss…' She stopped. Mortified.

Leo's tone had gone from angry to icy. 'You

could have informed me when I told you I was going to take you as my mistress.'

Angel looked up, stung, anger rising. To think that she was going through this humiliation *again*. 'How? Was I supposed to just come out with it?'

Leo just glared at her, a muscle popping in his jaw. Angel felt deflated all of a sudden. She backed away. Leo didn't let her escape his blistering gaze. 'Dammit, Angel you should have told me.'

He stilled then, and instinctively Angel grew wary. He asked silkily, 'Did you come back here to sleep with me after discussing your options with your father? Like some kind of sacrificial virgin?'

Horror rose from Angel's gut. She shook her head. 'No. *No*. How could you think such a thing? My father isn't even here, he's gone to London.'

Leo raked a hand through his hair, making it flop with unruly sexiness onto his forehead. Angel's belly clenched even now. She was aware of a pervading sense of hollow disappointment. Evidently he wasn't willing to sleep with her, to take her innocence. Suddenly she couldn't bear to be so vulnerable in front of him for a moment longer.

'I'm going to go back to my room.'

After a long moment Leo just nodded, and said darkly, 'I think that's a good idea.'

Leo watched Angel walk out of the room, the gaping dress showing the slender length of her smooth back in a curiously vulnerable way. He felt pole-axed. Winded. *She was a virgin*. Or was she? He cursed himself. As she'd said herself, it wouldn't take much to find out, and if he took her now, as he was aching to do, and she was telling the truth…he'd hurt her.

So if she was telling the truth she hadn't had countless lovers, hadn't been mistress to other men. It meant that his belief in one aspect of her behaviour had to be amended. For a second he again had the sickening suspicion that this was all part of some plan concocted with her father. Lead him on and drop the bombshell. But then he remembered the look of abject horror mixed with disgust on her face when he'd suggested that. It had been too real to ignore. She'd said her father hadn't even been there, and that would be easy enough to prove. Something uncomfortable lodged in Leo's chest.

He sat down on the edge of his bed and dropped his head for a moment. How the hell did someone like her remain a virgin till the age of twenty-four? For some reason he wasn't prepared to look too closely at why that might be.

He suddenly remembered when they'd been in the study the previous evening. He'd brought her to certain orgasm, or very close. He'd been disgusted to find himself so out of control in that moment. Bringing a fully-clothed woman to orgasm—a woman who had just been caught stealing from his family! At the time he'd dismissed her reaction, not believing it, thinking she was acting. But if her reaction had been genuine it would explain the shocked look on her face, her embarrassment.

Hadn't he felt compelled to pour her that drink? And then her agitation had led her to knock the glass out of his hand... Leo looked up again at the door she'd just walked through. The certainty hit him that she was telling the truth. You couldn't fake that kind of innocence.

He was angry—angry with himself for not noticing the signs. He was a connoisseur of women, and yet he'd kissed and held an innocent in his arms and hadn't even noticed. Because he'd been too inflamed. That was the truth. The minute he came within a foot of Angel his brain started to melt and hormones took over. Out of control. He grimaced. As evidenced by everything leading up to this moment.

When she'd stopped him it had taken more strength than he'd known he possessed to pull back from her lithe, firm body. He'd nearly exploded just seeing her breasts revealed, two beautifully shaped firm mounds, tipped with those small, hard nipples, enticing him to lick and explore.

Already the fire was building in his body again. And something else. The realisation that no other man had discovered the intimate secrets of Angel's body. A curious bubbling feeling made Leo's chest expand.

Leo realised that every other man they encountered in Athens might want Angel, but he would know that they hadn't been her lover… She was a virgin, and she was his. He had the power in his hands to make her uniquely his. Something deeply primitive within him thrilled at the sound of those words, at their implication…

To Angel's horror, as soon as she stepped under the spray of her shower, weak hot tears started falling down her cheeks, followed by gut-wrenching sobs. She pressed her hands to her face. She couldn't believe she was feeling this way. She couldn't believe that Leo, a man she barely knew, was so far under her skin that he had the power to hurt her like this, when she had every reason to hate him. How could she *want* someone like him to want her? Why wasn't she happy she'd scored a point? Even she had seen that she'd dented his insufferable confidence for one moment. Stopped him in his tracks…

Angel eventually turned off the shower and stepped out, shivering slightly despite the heat.

She roughly towel-dried her hair and pulled on a voluminous robe that was hanging on the back of the door, not even drying herself properly.

She felt flat and empty. Achilles had turned away from her in disgust when he'd discovered her virginity, when he'd known that she couldn't please him. But Achilles had been a boy. Leo Parnassus was a man. She'd been right to worry; it was so obvious now that he would want nothing to do with a novice.

Angel felt nauseous. Had he been so repulsed? But why else would he have stopped? For a man as virile as him to stop making love just because she was a virgin had to be because he had no interest in being her first lover… Angel couldn't contemplate for a second that it might have been because she'd genuinely caught him off guard. That there might have been an honourable intention behind it. To indulge in that line of thinking made all sorts of feelings emerge in Angel's belly; much easier to think of Leo being cruel, single-minded.

She had no idea how things would work now. Perhaps Leo would take lovers on the side while he paraded her in public as his mistress? Angel's heart constricted. No doubt that might be a further humiliation he'd appreciate when he came to consider it.

But the stark evidence that no man wanted to

sleep with her…*that Leo didn't want to sleep with her*…sapped her confidence totally—no matter how much she might try and pretend otherwise. Somehow the reason why she was here, the fact that this all stemmed from Leo's desire for revenge, seemed of little consequence right now.

She stepped out of her bathroom, turning the light off as she did so. For a moment she didn't notice anyone else in the dimly lit bedroom. Then she heard a muted sound and looked up, suddenly tense.

Leo stood there, just a few feet away, still in his jeans, the top button open, giving a tantalising glimpse of the dark hair which led—Angel gulped. Was she dreaming? Was she so pathetic?

Leo put out a hand. 'Come here, Angel.'

It was him. On numb legs, trying to ignore the renewed zinging of energy through her veins, Angel walked forward. She stopped a couple of feet away, still needing to protect herself. Just because he was here, it didn't mean anything.

But in that moment Leo closed the distance, stepped right up to Angel, took her face in his hands and kissed her. Her mouth opened on a shocked gasp and Leo took devastating advantage, tongue stabbing deep, stroking along hers, until Angel's legs felt weak and her hands went to Leo's waist to hold on. It was a sensual onslaught that impacted every cell in her body.

The feel of his hot satiny skin under her hands made them stretch out, trying to feel as much as she could. She couldn't begin to explain what had just happened; she was only capable of feeling. And, like a coward, she shut out the cacophony of voices in her head.

Eventually Leo pulled back, but not much. With a gesture that was almost tender he stroked Angel's damp hair behind one ear. And then, his eyes on hers, glittering darkly, he said, 'You're mine now, Angel, no one else's.'

Angel looked up and couldn't speak. The moment was too huge. Leo's hands came to the belt of her robe and pulled it open. She kept looking at him, drawing confidence from the way his eyes fell and flared when he took in her naked body. He pushed the robe off her shoulders and it fell at her feet with a quiet thump. Moisture pooled between her legs and she fought not to squirm.

And then Angel watched with a palpitating heart as Leo removed his jeans, *again.* He was as magnificent as she remembered. She suddenly wanted to reach out and touch him. As if reading her mind, Leo said throatily, 'Go on. Touch me, Angel.'

Hesitantly she put out her hand and, with her heart in her mouth, encircled it around his erection. She heard his swift intake of breath. It felt amazing to her, hot and silky, but with a steel core. Experimentally she moved her hand up and down, shocked when she felt him harden and swell even more in her hand. Leo expelled a long hiss of breath and Angel looked up. His face was tight, eyes black, cheekbones slashed with dark colour. The thought of him embedding himself *in her* was nearly too much to imagine.

He put his hand on hers and gently removed it. For a second Angel felt bewildered. She was doing it wrong. And then he said, 'If you keep touching me like that this will be over very quickly for both of us.'

Angel blushed and felt an absurd burst of relief. Leo took her by the hand and led her to the bed, gently pushed her down. She watched as he came over her, huge and dark and powerful. When he'd done this just a short while before she'd felt out of her depth and overwhelmed, but now…something had shifted. There was a gentleness about Leo that was desperately seductive.

As he took her mouth with his Angel arched herself into him, arms and hands searching to touch him, hold him. Their tongues collided feverishly, teeth nipping and biting. Angel could feel herself writhing underneath him, as if to try and feel every part of him.

Leo took his mouth away, and Angel gave a mewl of distress which quickly turned into a groan when she felt him cup one breast and bring the aching, tingling tip into the hot cavern of his mouth. Angel's back arched. Her hand stabbed into his hair.

His other hand was travelling up her leg, caressing, smoothing, feeling, until he spanned one thigh. Angel's legs fell open. He traced a path from her inner thigh to the juncture of her legs and she squirmed with intense pleasure.

His mouth moved to her other breast as his hand and fingers found that secret sweet spot between her legs, and she had to bite back a groan when she felt him stroke along plump and moistened folds. She was so wet.

Leo started to press hot kisses down her belly. Angel lifted her head, dizzy with desire and lust and an achy need for fulfilment. 'Leo... please...' She was not even sure what she was asking for.

'What, Angel?' He looked up, his voice sounding unbelievably husky, rough. 'What do you want?'

His fingers continued to tease, stroking her, making her hips twitch. And then, with a determined look in his eyes, he inserted two fingers inside her, going deeper, harder, and Angel gasped out loud. The feeling was so...intimate. Leo kept his hand where it was and moved up, his mouth hovering for a long moment just inches away from

Angel's breast, where a nipple pouted wantonly towards him.

Feeling emboldened, Angel arched her back, offering herself up, and with a feral smile Leo bent his head and flicked out his tongue, teasing that hard tip until it stood tight and erect. Angel's head fell back. His hand was between her legs, his tongue on her breast... The tightening, building deliciousness she'd felt before was happening again and she couldn't stop it, didn't want to.

Just when she hovered on the edge, about to tumble down, Leo took his hand from between her legs and moved away slightly. Angel let out a faint moan of despair. She heard the rustle of a package. A condom.

Then Leo was back and hovering over her. Broad and powerful. She could feel his body move between her legs.

'Open up more for me, Angel...'

Angel parted her legs, allowing Leo into the cradle of her hips. Holding himself in one hand, he allowed the tip of his sex to move along the wet heat of her arousal to see how ready she was. She felt a pulse throb down there and groaned. Her head went back. She could feel that smooth head, teasing along her slick folds, being moistened with her juices.

Her hips started to buck towards Leo; she wanted

him to impale her, but he drew back for a moment. His voice sounded rough. 'Patience, Angel…'

He bent down and covered her body with his, his chest crushing her breasts. Her nipples were like knife-points against him. Angel felt like sobbing out her frustration, but just then she felt Leo slide into her, his mouth coming over hers in as if to swallow her pain.

She gasped open-mouthed against him. The sting of pain was there, but not as she'd felt it before. He pulled back and looked down at her. 'Okay?'

Angel nodded.

She felt him push in a little further and winced. She could feel that she was so tight around him, but the awful dreaded pain wasn't lingering. It was slightly uncomfortable, yes, but very quickly that was being overtaken with something that felt amazing.

Angel's heart sang, and she said breathily, 'It's fine, Leo…it feels fine.'

In that moment Angel got a sense of how much Leo was holding back. She could see his shoulders shake slightly and his brow was beaded with sweat. With a deep groan Leo thrust all the way into her, and Angel gasped, her back arching on an instinct.

She couldn't speak. She felt so full, so *right*. So she spoke with her eyes and her hands, urging him to go on, to take up the rhythm, without even really knowing what she was doing or asking.

Leo pulled back and then thrust again, taking it slow and easy for the first few times, allowing Angel to get used to him. But then she felt an urgency build up within her. She wanted him to go harder, faster. She craved it. She was answering some deeply ancient call of the most feminine part of her. 'Please, Leo…'

'Yes, Angel, yes…stay with me.'

Leo answered her incoherent plea. With their bodies slick with sweat, he started to thrust into her, exactly as she craved with every atom of her being. Her hips jerked to meet his, to try and wring every drop out of him with each cataclysmic penetration of her body.

Then the pinnacle of every sensation she'd ever known was reached and transcended. She stopped breathing, her eyes on Leo's—did he know what was happening to her? He smiled as if he knew exactly what was happening, and with one powerful surge of his body into hers Angel was flung into another universe. A universe filled with exploding stars and a sweet, sweet oblivion.

Leo lay on his back, Angel tucked into his side, his arm around her. One long, smooth leg was thrown over his. He could feel her breasts pressing into him, those sweet, soft mounds tipped with those small, hard nipples. Even now he could still taste them on his tongue, their sweet muskiness.

Even though he'd taken her just a short time ago his body was ready for more. In fact he'd never been kept in such a state of arousal after making love. He could feel the unsteady beat of Angel's heart, slowly coming back to normal, and her breath was a little uneven. He knew that she'd fallen into a sleep of sorts.

Leo reeled. He'd had sex. Lots of sex. But nothing had come close to what he'd just experienced. He tried desperately to rationalise it: It had to be because she'd been a virgin. It had to be. Because if it wasn't—Angel moved. Leo's heart stopped; anticipation coiled deep inside him.

Angel was aware of consciousness returning slowly, trickling back. She was tucked into Leo's body, his arm tight around her, and everything rushed back in glorious Technicolor. She was a woman now. Leo hadn't rejected her. Immediately she could feel moist heat between her legs, readying her for him again.

Angel's hand moved down over Leo's chest, exploring the play of his powerful muscles underneath that exquisitely golden olive skin, the brush of hair that made her tingle all over. She could feel tension come into the muscles under her hand and smiled against his skin. She didn't want words, she couldn't speak; she just wanted him.

When her seeking hand found what she was looking for a fiercely feminine exultation ran through her at finding him so hard and ready. She lifted her head and Leo turned to face her. He looked serious, and a little shiver of something snaked down Angel's spine, but she quashed it. He put his hand over hers, stopping her movements.

'Angel…you're bound to be sore.'

She came up and shook her head, putting her finger to his lips. She did ache, but it was an ache that cried out for fulfilment, not an ache of pain. She took her other hand from him and guided his hand to the juncture between her legs where he could feel for himself how ready she was.

Leo said something that sounded guttural and then moved fast, so that Angel was on her back and he was looming over her, already moving between her legs. The ache was building at her core, and if Angel could have stopped and slowed time in that moment, she would have.

'Yes, Leo…this is what I want…please.'

He bent his head said close to her mouth, 'Well, since you ask so nicely…'

When Angel woke again, the curtains were open and sunlight flooded her room. For a second everything was a blank. And then she became aware of certain *aches* and sensations in her body that weren't usual. As her consciousness returned fully everything came back in glorious Technicolor, and her heart tripped before starting up again at double speed. She knew that Leo wasn't in the bed; she'd somehow known that immediately.

It stunned her slightly to know how quickly her life had changed one hundred and eighty degrees. This time yesterday *she'd still been a virgin*.

Last night Leo had made her a woman. He'd taken her to a paradise she'd never dreamed existed. Heat suffused Angel from head to toe. And yet she couldn't stop a smile from breaking across her face. It was impossible to ignore the fact that her body felt as if it had been awoken from a deep, cold sleep...

But just as quickly her smile faded again, when the enormity of it all sank in. How could she be feeling like this for someone who had so coldly set out to take her because he wanted her and wanted to punish her? She frowned minutely, staring at the ceiling. She felt confused; Leo had taken her innocence with such devastating generosity that she reeled. Several times she'd seen the strain of his efforts to hold back, as if he was afraid he'd hurt her.

Angel lifted the sheet and looked into the bed,

ignoring the signs of having been seriously seduced on her body, the faint bruises and reddish marks. There was no blood. Angel let the sheet drop; she knew rationally that there wasn't always necessarily blood, but there was a stinging between her legs that spoke of the potential of it if Leo hadn't been so gentle. And yet she could remember the desperation with which she'd urged him on, even when he'd tried to hold back for her sake.

With a burgeoning feeling of something huge in her chest Angel got out of bed and pulled on the robe which still lay on the floor. To think of how Leo had pushed it off her shoulders with such singular intent made Angel blush all over again.

Without really thinking of what she was doing, Angel went to the door that connected their rooms. After hesitating for the merest moment, she turned the handle and went in.

She stumbled to a halt when she saw Leo standing at the mirror of his wardrobe, knotting a tie. His eyes merely flicked to her through the mirror and then back to his task, with no change in expression. She hadn't been sure what to expect, but it hadn't been that. Angel was immediately tongue-tied. Leo looked so distant and intimidating in a dark suit, white shirt and tie. He looked like the phenomenally successful businessman he was. And nothing like the tender lover of last night. She suddenly knew she'd been an abject fool.

His eyes flicked to Angel again, and she felt heat rise in her face when she registered how cool they were. One dark brow rose quizzically. 'Was there something you wanted, Angel?'

Was there something you wanted, Angel? Angel balked and died a tiny death in that moment. Was this the same man? Acting as if the most cataclysmic thing on the earth hadn't just happened? But then, she realised in sick horror, it hadn't—not for him. If anything, last night for him must have been excruciatingly banal. How could it not have been, with a complete innocent?

She shook her head vaguely. 'I just…' *I just what?* she mocked herself bitterly, cursing her impulse to come in here. How could she have disregarded everything that lay between them, forgotten why she was there?

A lot of things were impacting upon Angel, all at the same time. Leo turned from the mirror, his tie perfectly knotted, his shoulders broad and awesome in the jacket, hair smoothed back, jaw clean shaven. Aloof.

Very quickly Angel assessed the situation, her brain working overtime. She brought her hands to her robe and tightened it, barely registering the way Leo's eyes dropped there for a split second.

She tipped up her chin, forcing her voice to be cool. 'I was just wondering what time the stylist will be here? You did say that you'd have someone come today?'

Leo's jaw clenched and he strolled nonchalantly towards Angel, barely leashed power in every step. A flash of memory—those muscular thighs between hers last night—made a light sweat break out over Angel's top lip. She fought not to retreat, not to show that she was barely holding it together in the face of his obvious distance. He stopped a few feet away, his gaze sweeping up and down in a blistering moment that nearly scuppered Angel's precious composure.

'You were an eager student last night, Angel. I can see our time together being most…enjoyable.'

Angel burned inside. With humiliation and, more treacherously, with hurt, in response to his whole demeanour and his calling her *eager*. She had been desperately, awfully eager. She had fallen into his bed more easily than a ripe apple falling from a tree. She wanted to lash back, and hitched her chin a mite higher.

'I wouldn't know, as I have so little experience to compare it to. But for what it's worth last night was…pleasant enough.'

Leo laughed out loud, a big burst of sound that made Angel flinch. When he looked at her his eyes flashed a warning, and a mocking smile played around his sensual mouth. Angel had to fight against the pull in her belly, the desire to just stop and look at it. She dragged her gaze back up to his.

He stepped even closer and put out a hand, touching her jaw. Angel clenched it.

'Sweetheart, I know exactly how it was for you. I felt every ripple of every one of your orgasms, so don't pretend that it was anything less than *pleasant*.'

Angel knocked his hand away, dying somewhere inside. 'Like I said, you'd know so much more than me. I'm sure the novelty won't last long.'

Leo calmly replaced his hand, taking a firmer grip on Angel's jaw. 'On the contrary,' he drawled, 'I don't see this novelty fading for some time. You're all fire underneath that angelic exterior, and I'm looking forward to seeing a lot more of it. This is only the beginning.'

With that, he dropped his hand and stepped back. Angel thought for a split second that she saw some chink in his composure, and it had her heart beat hard in response. But then he looked at his watch and said crisply, 'The stylist will be here at noon, followed by someone to give you some beauty treatments. We've got our first public outing tonight, Angel—a ball to celebrate my taking over Parnassus Shipping as CEO. It should be fun for you. It's at the Grand Bretagne, where you're more intimately acquainted with the dirty sheets. I'll be back later. Wear something appropriate for your first viewing as my mistress.'

He ran a finger down her hot cheek. 'I'm looking forward to stirring things up with you by my side.'

CHAPTER SIX

As Leo sat in a meeting in his new boardroom later that day, to his utter chagrin he found he wasn't concentrating on the discussion—which didn't disturb him too much; he was already two steps ahead of everyone else in the room. All he could think about was Angel and last night. And how she'd looked this morning when she'd come into his room, the lurch he'd felt in his chest when he'd seen her hesitation. How hard it had been to stand there and see her softly flushed face, those huge blue eyes, and not rip her robe from her body and spread her underneath him again.

His body was tight with arousal even now—*not* a state he welcomed in the middle of the day, surrounded by work colleagues, and with Ari Levakis looking at him with a small frown. Leo smiled.

But it was futile. He kept getting flashes of moments: when he'd thrust into her for the first time and heard that telltale indrawn gasp, how tight she'd clamped around him, how sweetly she'd opened up for him, allowing him to sink deeper and deeper. How her skin had tasted, like sweet musk and crushed roses.

Like sweet musk and crushed roses? Leo gave himself an inner shake. He had to get it together. Angel Kassianides was a piece of work.

For a moment that morning he'd thought that he'd seen something achingly vulnerable in her face, and it had made him close up inside. Close up against the inevitable attempt of a woman to turn intimacy into something emotional. But then, when he'd walked over to her, she'd been composed and cool. So much so that he knew he'd be a fool if he trusted any of her reactions for a moment.

She was his mistress, she was *his*, and the thought of the evening to come, when he could parade her in public and know that he was her only lover, was tantalising in the extreme.

Angel sat beside Leo in the back of his car later that evening. Her throat ached with a huge lump. She hated the fact that she was so raw about what had happened. All day she'd not been able to get out of her head the coolness Leo had subjected her to that morning. Right now, she didn't think she could ever let him touch her again, but just then, as if to mock her assertion, she felt a big hand close over hers, where it lay on her leg, and her blood started to speed up.

'You look beautiful tonight.'

Angel exerted iron control over her emotions and turned slowly to face Leo, not a hint of her inner turmoil showing on her face. She smiled and it felt brittle. 'Well, you paid enough for it.'

Leo's eyes were dark, with those golden lights lurking in their depths, already undoing some of Angel's rigid control. She left her hand lax in his, even though she wanted desperately to pull away. His dark tuxedo elevated his appeal to another level. And he just said, softly now, while shaking his head, 'Money has nothing to do with true beauty. And you are, Angel, truly beautiful.'

Leo found that he was saying the words with a reverent sincerity that he couldn't help. When he'd walked into her room earlier he hadn't known what to expect. His heart had beaten a curious tattoo, and he'd found that his chest had been tight with anticipation. She'd been standing at her window, slender back to him. He'd seen many women, in many beautiful gowns for his pleasure, but none he'd ever seen had taken his breath away before they'd even turned around.

The dress was floor length, and a deeply turquoise colour. Silk. Apart from that Leo hadn't known much, because he'd felt dizzy with lust. It draped and fell in such a way as to turn her into some sort of goddess creature. Her hair was twisted up and held in place by a flower of a similar colour to the dress.

Disgusted with his reaction, he'd had to call her name to get her to turn around, and she'd done so, so slowly it had had the effect of a striptease on his body, even when she was fully clothed!

Her breasts were lovingly caressed by the silk of the dress, the deep V between them a shadow of promise. Her head had been high, chin tipped up in a gesture that had seemed almost defiant. It had been all Leo could do to stand still and extend an autocratic hand, gesturing her to come to him. And when she'd walked, and the soft silk had swirled around her body—

Leo came back to the present and shifted uncomfortably in the back of the car.

For a second the cool and controlled woman suddenly looked slightly unsure. And Leo reacted. What was he doing, all but drooling over her like this? His hand tightened on hers for a second, and he felt the small delicate bones, the slight roughness of her skin that hinted at the work she'd been doing, and his chest tightened again for a second.

He thrust aside all the nebulous feelings he didn't understand, and asked, 'How do you think your father will react to seeing us together when he gets the papers tomorrow? Because this is going to be all over the world, Angel…'

Angel shivered and tried to pull her hand away, but Leo held it tight. She hated him in that moment. Really hated him. The only thing stopping her from trying to jump out of the car as it idled at a set of lights was the memory of the ecstatic phone call she'd had from Delphi earlier, telling her that she would be marrying Stavros in a month's time. And also the surprise that Angel had felt at Leo acting on his word so soon.

Her voice was unaccountably husky, with all the confusing emotions rushing through her. 'I think you know very well how he'll react. He'll be apoplectic. He'll be utterly humiliated.'

Leo lifted a brow, speculation all over his face. 'Will he, though, Angel? Or have you and he planned exactly this all along?'

Hating feeling so cornered and mistrusted, Angel hit back. 'What if we have? You'll never know, will you?'

Leo moved close and Angel arched back, but it was no good. Leo's hand came out and caressed the back of her neck. His other hand came up and cupped her silk-covered breast. She hadn't been able to wear a bra, and she was horrified to feel her nipple peak and thrust against the silk. His thumb moved lazily against her nipple and Angel bit back a moan. *How* could he have this effect on her?

'I'll know, Angel, because from now on, until I'm bored with you, I'll know every move you make. So any plans you and he have cooked up will be futile.'

'But we don't—'

Her words were crushed under Leo's mouth and everything disappeared into a haze of urgent desire. Since he'd come into her room earlier, when she'd not even been able to turn around to face him until he'd called her name, finally doing so with her heart beating so loud he had to have heard it, Angel had, in some deep and traitorous place wanted to feel his mouth on hers again.

And now it was, and she was being sucked under all over again. Mindlessly helpless to fight him. She wasn't aware of the car drawing to a halt, or the driver clearing his throat. She was only aware of Leo pulling back, and her gasping in of breath when she opened her eyes and tried to focus. Her body felt jittery and on fire. Leo just smiled at her, triumph in his gaze, and Angel could only watch as his eyes travelled down and took in the obvious state of her arousal, her nipples as hard as berries, standing out starkly against the unforgiving silk.

'Perfect.'

And before Angel knew what he meant Leo was out of the car, coming around to open her door and pulling her out. She still felt dizzy, spaced out, and then there was nothing but Leo's hand around hers and a barrage of lights and questions. She'd just become Leo's very public property.

Later, Angel sat in her chair and felt thoroughly out of place. She'd been away at boarding school for so long, and then at college, so that she'd never really integrated into Athens society. Her mouth twisted. Well, not the way Leo believed, anyway. Despite that, she did know people in the room, and she saw their looks and their whispering and she hated that it affected her. She'd gone to the bathroom earlier, and heard two women talking by the sinks.

'Can you *believe* he came with her?'

'I know. I mean, no one would be surprised if he crossed to the other side of the street to ignore her and that awful family after what they did…'

The other woman had laughed nastily. 'Can't you just imagine her buffoon of a father's face if he saw them together? I wouldn't be surprised if Leo Parnassus is only taking her as some sort of revenge. He's practically ignored her all evening…'

The other woman had sighed lustily then, and said, 'I wouldn't mind him taking me for revenge… Obviously he sees something in her too-innocent-to-be-true face.'

The stinging words came back to Angel now, and she held her head up high and gritted her teeth. This was all part of Leo's plan. Ritual humiliation.

Just then Angel saw Lucy Levakis return to the table where they'd been seated. She was the English wife of Aristotle Levakis, Leo's business partner, and the only person who'd been genuinely sweet to Angel—no doubt because she didn't know of the history. Ari Levakis, though, had been sending her dark speculative looks all night, clearly of the same mind as Leo, and suspicious of her motives. After all, he'd been one of the people she'd recognised at that party in the villa all those weeks ago. Angel felt sick. Did he know about Leo's revenge?

Lucy sat down and said chattily, 'You looked lonely over here, so I thought I'd come and join you. Honestly, *men*—they get so wrapped up in themselves.'

Angel smiled tightly. She didn't want to taint this nice woman with her dubious reputation. 'Really, I don't mind if you want to go back. I'm fine here.'

Lucy shook her head, and just then Angel noticed something and felt her heart lift for the first time in days. She'd obviously not noticed before, too preoccupied with everything. She sat forward and asked shyly, 'That necklace you're wearing, where did you get it?'

Lucy beamed and told Angel all about how Ari had known how much she loved it and had proposed to her with it. 'To this day I don't own an engagement ring.' She touched the necklace reverently. 'This is my engagement ring.'

Angel smiled, blushing with pride. 'I designed that necklace.'

Lucy gasped. 'You *what*?'

Angel nodded. 'I did jewellery design at college, and that was the only piece I sold from my graduation show. I gave the rest of the collection to my sister and some friends as gifts.'

Lucy gasped again, 'But you could have made a fortune!'

Angel was aware of the irony. It had been shortly after her graduating that their personal circumstances had changed so dramatically. She hadn't known that she'd have to turn her back on her dream profession so soon, otherwise she might have kept her collection intact. She smiled now, ruefully. 'I preferred to give it away.'

Lucy said something incoherent, and before she knew it Angel's hand had been grabbed and she was being dragged in the taller woman's wake over to the men. She tried to remonstrate with her but to no avail.

Angel heard her interrupt them excitedly and explain what Angel had just revealed. Angel looked up to see Ari's *very* speculative gaze and then, gulping, looked at Leo. His eyes showed no emotion. No doubt he thought she might be lying. Lucy gave a groan then, when she realised the time, and said she'd have to go home to relieve their nanny. Angel had learned that they had two small children.

Her heart clenched when she saw Ari's attention go back to his wife and he pulled her close, making his excuses too, despite Lucy's insistence that he stay. Clearly the man couldn't wait to be alone with his wife, and Angel's heart clenched even harder.

They made their goodbyes, Lucy still excited to have discovered Angel's secret, and then they were gone. Angel expected Leo to make an excuse and leave her alone again, and she had even started walking back to the table when Leo caught her hand and pulled her back.

She looked up at him.

'Where do you think you're going?'

'I…' Angel faltered, and cursed herself for being so weak. She felt a fire of rebellion start to build. 'I was going back to the table to sit alone again, so that everyone can see how you ignore me. But actually, now that the speeches are over, the dais is so much more public. Why don't I just go up and sit there? I could even put a sign around my neck if you wish—'

'Stop it.'

Angel couldn't, too hurt. 'Why, Leo? Isn't this exactly what you planned? A round of public appearances with your mistress of revenge, making it perfectly obvious that your only interest in me is completely superficial? Making sure there is maximum speculation, maximum humiliation?'

Angel bit her lip. The words had spilled out before she could stop them. 'Well, if it's any consolation, the gossip in the powder room is already rife, and let's just say I don't come off well.'

Leo frowned. 'What did you hear?'

Angel shook her head, aghast at having revealed so much. 'It doesn't matter.'

Because the awful thing was, he might be humiliating her in public, but he'd be taking her to bed at night, and once in his bed the last thing she felt was humiliated.

Leo opened his mouth to speak, but just then someone came to interrupt them. Much to Angel's surprise, he didn't let go of her hand; he kept her close, introducing her to the other man. And, while he didn't go out of his way to include her in the conversation, he didn't let her out of his sight for the rest of the evening, making Angel's emotions see-saw even more.

In the car on the way home, Angel rotated her

head to try and ease out the kinks. She was exhausted.

'Did you really design Lucy's necklace?'

Angel stopped rotating her head and looked at Leo warily. 'Of course. I wouldn't lie about something like that. What would be the point?'

Her simple assertion struck him somewhere deep. Leo just looked at her for a long moment. 'It's a beautiful piece.'

Angel shrugged awkwardly. He sounded surprised, as if he hadn't meant to give her a compliment. 'Thank you.'

'You haven't been making jewellery since you left college because…?'

Angel jumped in. This was a very tender point for her. 'I haven't been making jewellery because I don't have the facilities.'

Leo shook his head. 'But you've been working, surely it's possible to rent a workspace?'

'The equipment and the raw materials I need are too expensive.'

Leo sat back. 'You must really resent having had to resort to menial work.'

Angel blinked. In that moment she realised that she'd never resented having to work; she'd only missed the fact that she'd had to put off her dream. It had been very simple: she'd had to be there for Delphi. Necessitating that they stay at home to cut down on living costs. She shook her head. 'I had no choice.'

Leo found himself wondering uncomfortably why Angel hadn't just resorted to hanging out on the vibrant Athenian social scene in order to try and seduce a rich husband from her own social sphere. Evidently her sister had done just that… But then just as quickly he found himself quashing the curiosity when he found it inevitably led to wondering how she'd remained a virgin. A virgin didn't go out to seduce rich husbands.

She wasn't a virgin any more; she was *his*. Something deeply primitive and possessive moved through him. Ruthlessly he pulled Angel over until she sat in his lap. She resisted him, but he caressed her back through the flimsy silk. He'd seen her sitting alone at their dinner table earlier, and had had to restrain himself from going over and claiming her. The only thing that had stopped him had been the weakness he'd felt that would show, especially when Ari Levakis had been quizzing him as to why on earth he'd taken her as his mistress. So he'd let her sit there, but had been burningly aware of her every second, of the proud way she'd held her head— defiant, almost.

It hadn't sat well with him, and when Angel had said those things to him he'd felt shame clawing upwards. Not an emotion he was used to when it came to women.

No matter why he was with Angel, he'd had no conscious intention of ignoring her in public. His plan had been humiliation, yes, but that would come when he had had enough of her and ejected her from his life, making it very clear she'd been just a temporary addition. It would come from knowing that Tito Kassianides would be confronted with pictures splashed all over the tabloids tomorrow of his daughter in bed with the enemy.

In truth, he'd been shocked to hear her say that she'd already been the subject of gossip; clearly Athens was in a league with New York and its wildfire gossip circuit.

Angel still resisted him on his lap, looking resolutely out of the window. He stroked her back and pressed an open-mouthed kiss against her arm. He felt the first tiny signs of her relaxing and smiled. His caressing hand pulled her in closer, until she fell against him, yet still she was tense. His other hand rested on her thigh and then started to move to where her legs were pressed tightly together.

With gentle force he pressed his hand against her *mons*. He could feel heat coming through the silk, and the inevitable hardening of his own arousal. He moved subtly and heard Angel's indrawn breath as she felt him push against the thin barrier of her dress, against the globes of her bottom.

He reached up and pulled her chin around to face him. He didn't like the look in her eyes: it was too *naked*. Too full of things he didn't want to know. So he pulled her head down and kissed her, hard, and with a deep groan of triumph felt her sink into him completely, her lithe body pressing into his, enflaming him so much that by the time they reached the villa he was aching to bury himself inside her.

By the end of that first week the whole world knew that Leo Parnassus had taken Angel as his mistress. Paparazzi were camped at the gates to the villa. Every night they'd gone out, either to a function or just for dinner, and the response had been a growing hysteria.

Headlines screamed out of newsstands: *'Parnassus and Kassianides bury seventy years of enmity between the sheets.'* And other headlines, more snide, with suggestions of Leo Parnassus being paid *in kind*. It was awful. It was exactly what Leo had planned.

One morning, when Angel had gone down to breakfast and had been surprised to see Leo there, she'd asked nervously, 'What about your father—won't this hurt him?'

Leo had looked at her sharply, and then with a hard look had said, 'My father is aware of the situation, but he has no say in who I choose as my lover.'

Angel had swallowed nervously, unaccountably concerned for the much elder man she could remember seeing at the party in the villa; he'd looked so *frail*. 'But still, it can't be easy, when he's spent his whole life wanting to avenge his family name.'

Leo had just replied with silken emphasis, 'Which is exactly what I'm doing. My father, above all things, is a strategist. If he knew for a second what you'd done, what a threat you are, he would endorse my methods wholeheartedly.'

Angel had still felt miserable to think of how his father might be feeling, and had been reminded again that whenever Leo spoke of him it was clear that little love was lost.

And then Leo had asked casually, 'Have you spoken to *your* father yet?'

Angel had blanched and shaken her head. She knew from Delphi that her father was home and in a near constant state of violent inebriation, cursing her volubly. His trip to London had been spectacularly unsuccessful. Angel knew a lot of his bluster was just that. And she wasn't scared for Delphi's safety. Her father had only ever lashed out at her, Angel, with his fists, in those moments when she reminded him too much of her mother.

She'd shaken her head again. 'No, we haven't spoken.' Angel sent up a silent prayer. At least when Delphi was married she'd be moving in with Stavros and Angel would be free to live elsewhere. And lick her wounds from the fall-out of her association with Leo.

Leo had looked suspicious. Angel had done her best to ignore him.

Now, Angel sighed as she looked in the full-length mirror of her dressing room. She was tired. And she had to admit that she was still shell-shocked. She felt as though from the moment she'd met Leo again, that fateful night in the study, she'd not had a chance to draw breath.

He consumed her utterly. In the nights he taught her body how it could respond so powerfully to his; but she was still shy, still mortified at her reaction to him. And her days were filled with vivid flashbacks to moments that took her breath away, making her body heat up and melt all over again.

She quite literally could not remember what it had been like not to know this man, not to know his hard features, the faint line of the scar above his mouth which still tantalised her.

She tried to clear her mind of him and twisted in front of the mirror. The dress she wore was the most daring one yet. It was strapless and mostly gold, ending a few inches above her knees, where the gold tapered off into silver. Her waist was cinched in with a gold belt, and gold hoop earrings and strappy sandals completed the outfit.

Something defiant had made her pick it out of the myriad clothes that now filled the walk-in closet, along with a glittering array of stunning jewellery. When she'd seen the jewellery her heart had twisted. How she longed to make her own again. She'd always found the designs of others too garish for her tastes, preferring delicate chains and subtle designs. Like Lucy's butterfly necklace.

She heard a sound, and whirled around to see Leo, leaning nonchalantly against her door, already dressed and ready to go. She felt vulnerable at having been observed. This was how it seemed to be going. He'd be gone every day to work when she awoke, her body heavy after the rigours of a long night of lovemaking. Then he'd come home and get ready, only coming to fetch her when she too was ready. Minimal conversation. Minimal emotional involvement.

She'd noticed Leo tensing beside her last night, at an art gallery opening, when a couple had started a passionate and very public row. When Angel had glanced up at him in response to his hand tightening on hers, she'd been surprised to see him looking slightly mesmerised, and yet grey underneath his tan. Eventually he'd turned from the scene, with disgust etched all over his face. Angel hadn't been able to understand his reaction; it had seemed totally disproportionate to what was really just a domestic fight.

She found that the memory and the concern she'd felt now made her feel even more vulnerable. She didn't care about what made Leo tick. She only cared that he was facilitating her sister's happiness.

She drew on all the confidence she could and put a hand on her hip, cocking her head. 'Well? Is it suitably mistressy for you?'

Leo's jaw clenched, and Angel's belly quivered.

'Don't push me, Angel.' His eyes dropped then insultingly, lingering and assessing. He looked at her again, and all her bravado had melted.

He just said cuttingly, 'Yes, it's perfect. Exactly the kind of thing the press will be expecting you to wear. Let's go.'

CHAPTER SEVEN

IN THE car on the way down to Athens, Leo fought back waves of anger and irritation. The sight of Angel's smooth thighs out of the corner of his eye was nearly too much.

When he'd first seen her in the dress he'd wanted to march in and rip it off her. To find something much more suitable, something that might cover her from head to toe. To his utter shock and ignominy, it had only been when she'd turned around and been so provocatively cocky that he'd realised his desire to change it stemmed from somewhere very ambiguous.

He'd suddenly been uncomfortable with the idea of her going out and looking so obviously like his mistress. When that was exactly what he wanted. The fact that he'd had to remind himself of that fact struck hard now. Also, more worryingly, sleeping with Angel for the past week had done nothing to diminish her effect on him. Every time he slept with her, thrust into her lissom body, his desire increased exponentially. He'd also been growing acutely aware of the attention Angel garnered from other men, attention she *appeared* not to notice, but he didn't trust her for a second.

He was embarking on a new path, taking up residence in his ancestral home, not to mention taking control of a multi-million-dollar organisation while keeping track of his own business concerns in New York. He had a million and two things to occupy his time and energy, not least of which was being vigilant and mindful of the vulnerabilities of his company in its time of transition.

He couldn't help feeling, with the space that Angel took up in his every waking moment, that he was being incredibly stupid. Willingly taking his enemy into his bed, where she was fast proving to have more control over him than he cared to admit.

The only way Leo knew to counter these doubts was to exert his own control, and right now he only wanted control of one thing: Angel. With a growl he ordered the driver to put up the privacy partition, and turned to reach for Angel in the exact moment that she turned to him with a question in her eyes.

The minute she saw him a delicate flush bloomed in her cheeks. He saw her eyes dilate and, without speaking a word, he pulled her over to straddle his lap. He pushed her short dress up over her thighs so that her legs could move more freely.

Leo gripped her waist then, moving her strategically, so that she could feel where he ached most. He was rewarded with a gasp, but Angel's eyes were curiously unemotional, as if she had locked herself away somewhere. To his utter consternation Leo found that thought repulsive. How dared she try and hide herself from him? She was *his*— mind, body and soul.

What ensued was a battle of wills more than an act of lovemaking, although it was that too. Explosively, with ruthless intent, Leo drew down his zip and pulled Angel's panties aside, and surged up into her moist heat.

He wouldn't let her look away. Every time she turned her face he ruthlessly brought it back. She closed her eyes, but he ground out, 'Open your eyes, Angel, *look* at me.'

And she did. With defiance blazing. It only served to make their lovemaking even more intense. Eyes locked. Angel clearly knew that Leo wanted something of her, and she was determined not to give it. Finally the moment came, and Leo could bear it no more. His body was screaming for release, Angel's moans had got more and more fractured, and he could feel the start of the spasms of her orgasm. He knew as soon as he felt it that he couldn't last. And he didn't.

For a long moment in the aftermath Leo's head rested on Angel's still covered breast. Their bodies intimately joined. He felt every last pulsating clench of her body around his. But it was only when he felt her hesitate for a second and then bring her hand up to stroke his hair that he realised he'd won that particular round. Curiously, though, he felt no sense of victory.

That night, at yet another function—Angel wondered desperately how much anyone could endure of this endless posturing and preening and networking—she was trying desperately not to give in to the temptation to tug her dress down over her legs, feeling exposed and angry with herself for choosing it now. She'd been too angry to change when Leo had declared that it was *perfect*.

What had happened in the car on the way there… She still burned at knowing she'd just let Leo do that. She'd done her best to remain aloof. But that was near impossible.

She'd learnt her lesson that first morning after they'd slept together. When he'd been so cold. Each night since then he'd come to her bed and they'd made love, but within minutes of finishing he'd get up and walk, naked, back to his own room.

No hanging around. No nice words. No cuddles or, God forbid, tenderness. No whispers in the night, talking of inane things, which was how she'd always imagined it might be with a lover.

'You're a million miles away, Angel.'

Angel's focus came back into the packed ballroom of one of Athens' plushest hotels. Lucy Levakis was looking at her with a teasing smile.

'Not that I blame you, of course,' she whispered then, with a pointed glance in the direction of the two men who conversed nearby, both tall and both commanding lots of attention—mostly female.

Lucy sighed indulgently as she looked at her husband. 'I can remember what it's like…' she said, and then, dryly, 'Who am I kidding? He still makes the rest of the room fade away.'

Angel smiled tightly. Ari had greeted her with more warmth tonight, as if she'd passed some silent test. Angel had fleetingly and far too wistfully wondered what it might take to break through Leo's wall of mistrust. She thought of how he'd caught her red-handed in his office, and had to concede it would take a lot. A belief that she could possibly be innocent when he had no reason whatsoever to believe otherwise, and zero interest.

Angel forced her thoughts away from that now, stung that she was feeling so vulnerable. She forced herself to smile more widely at Lucy. 'Anyone would think you two were still on your honeymoon, not going home to two small children.'

Just then Lucy got pulled aside by an acquaintance, so Angel was left on her own again, with Lucy sending back an apologetic grimace. Immediately, though, Leo turned his head where he stood with Ari a few feet away and held out a hand. With an awful lurching in her chest Angel reached out and took it, feeling as if something slightly momentous had just occurred. Which was ridiculous. But she realised in that moment that Leo hadn't once left her on her own since that first function. While he'd not exactly been demonstrative, he'd been solicitous and attentive.

But to be faced with Leo and Ari was nearly too much. They both packed a punch, even if Leo was the only one who made Angel's pulse race and her legs turn to jelly. She tried to ignore him and smiled at Ari, shyly asking about his and Lucy's children.

Ari rolled his eyes and groaned, 'Zoe is walking as of this week, so with her and Cosmo underfoot it's like an assault course. Just getting through the day and keeping them both alive is a feat in itself. Running a shipping fleet is a piece of cake in comparison.'

Angel smiled, inordinately relieved to see that Ari seemed to have definitely thawed towards her. She wondered if it was Lucy's influence.

Ari looked at Leo briefly, and then back to Angel, 'Actually, I have a favour to ask of you.'

Angel nodded. 'Sure, anything.'

'I'd like to commission you to make a set of jewellery for Lucy. Our anniversary is in a couple of months, and since she's found out that you designed the necklace I gave her I know she'd love a complete set. I was thinking of a bracelet, and perhaps earrings to match?'

Angel felt a dart of pure pleasure go through her, and she blushed. 'Well, I'm honoured that you'd ask… I'd love to do something…'

But then, just as suddenly, her spirits dropped like a stone when she realised that she had no way of being able to take on such a commission. 'But unfortunately I'm not really in a position at the moment to make anything new… I don't have the—'

'I'll make sure she has everything she might need.'

Angel's mouth opened and closed and she looked up at Leo, genuinely stymied.

Ari was already responding. 'Great. Angel, can you come to my office tomorrow morning and we can discuss the designs?'

Angel looked back to Ari, feeling as if the wind had just been knocked out of her. 'Yes, of course.'

Lucy returned then, and reminded him that they'd promised to be home by a certain time. As they left,

Ari gave Angel a discreet wink. When they'd gone, Angel looked up at Leo and said stiffly, 'You shouldn't have promised Ari that I could take the commission. You've no idea how expensive it might be to make what he wants, especially if he wants it so soon. Plus, I've no workspace.'

Leo pulled her into him, and that little move set off a host of butterflies in Angel's chest. Apart from holding her hand, Leo rarely touched her more intimately in public. 'The villa has a million empty rooms, and I've no intention of denying my friend what he wants.'

Why did her heart ache when his easy generosity to his friend was so apparent?

Angel stood at the door of the room, which had been found at the very back of the villa, and shook her head wryly. This was what untold limitless wealth did: it gave you a state-of-the-art jewellery-making workshop within days.

She walked in and touched the wooden table reverently, seeing the myriad tools and expensive metals and stones she'd listed for Leo all laid out. She hadn't had access to facilities and equipment so fine even in college. It gave her a pain in her heart to know that just as quickly Leo would have it ripped out and replaced by the generic room it had once been when the time came. She sighed deeply.

'Don't you like it?'

Angel whirled around, her hand going to her chest. 'You scared me half to death, creeping up on me like that!' But, even so, her treacherous body was already responding to the way Leo lounged so nonchalantly against the door, hands in the pockets of his trousers, shirt open at his throat.

'You look as if someone has just died, so the only thing I can deduce is that you hate your workshop.'

Angel shook her head, aghast that he'd seen her turmoil so easily. 'No, I love it.' She turned away, so he wouldn't see how vulnerable she felt to be caught like this. 'You must have spent a fortune on it.'

She turned back then, feeling more in control, and saw Leo shrug. 'I just told them to install the best.'

Angel smiled, feeling hurt at his nonchalance. 'Well, you got the best. I just hope it won't cost too much to rip it all out again.'

For a long moment he said nothing, and then, 'You don't have to concern yourself with that.'

Leo felt a surge of something rip through him at her casual words. She just stood there, in jeans and a T-shirt, looking so effortlessly sexy that he felt weak inside. He heard himself say harshly, 'Don't get any ideas about Ari Levakis, he's a happily married man.'

The look of sheer incomprehension on Angel's

face made Leo want to alternately shake her for acting and kick himself for being so obvious. But something about the way Ari had visibly warmed towards Angel, evident in the fact that he'd asked her for this commission, had sent something ominously dark into Leo's belly the other night.

He could remember the look of pure happiness on Angel's face when she'd returned from meeting Ari at his office to discuss the designs. For some reason Leo had decided to stay at home to work that day, and he'd walked into the hall when he'd heard her return. She'd been humming. But the minute she'd seen him her face had changed to wariness. She'd stopped humming.

Leo had walked over to her and all but dragged her into his study, where a passion like nothing he'd ever experienced before had made him take her on the edge of his desk like a hormonal teenager.

Now she just looked at him, her mouth looking bruised. Her eyes looking bruised. With *hurt*?

'I am well aware that Ari is a happily married man, and I can assure you that even if I had designs on the man, which I do not, he'd be about as likely to look at me twice as you will ever believe I'm innocent of trying to steal from you.'

Leo's chest tightened. 'Which is impossible.'

She hitched in a little breath, barely perceptible, but he'd heard it. 'Exactly' was all she said, but with a curious resignation in her voice. Almost defeated.

Later, when they returned from the opening night of a new restaurant, exhaustion was creeping over Angel in earnest. That little exchange in the jewellery workshop earlier had taken more out of her than she cared to admit. She was caught in such a bind. Apart from the fact that if she was ever to defend herself to Leo about that night in the study he'd have to trust her word, at this stage she was all too aware of Delphi's wedding looming on the horizon, and how important it was that nothing jeopardise it. Defending herself was futile. She was angry with herself for even wanting to be able to do so. For even feeling the need. As if Leo would ever show her another side of himself. She was damned because of who she was, no matter what.

She trailed Leo up the main staircase, hardly able to lift her head. She even bumped into him at the top of the stairs and gave out a yelp of fear when she felt herself falling backwards into thin air.

In a second Leo had turned and caught her, hauling her into his body. He looked down at her, frowning. 'What is the matter with you?'

Angel shook her head. Despite the aching tiredness, she could already feel the predictable response heating up in her body. Stirring it to life. 'Nothing, I'm just…a little tired.'

Leo continued to look down at her, until Angel started to squirm uncomfortably in his arms. Abruptly he let her go and backed away. Angel felt curiously bereft, and nearly fell down in shock when Leo just said, 'Go to bed, Angel. I have some calls to make to New York. I'll be on the phone for a couple of hours.'

Angel nodded, and tried not to acknowledge the stab of disappointment low down in her belly. Just before she turned away she stopped and said, 'I'm going to be out all day tomorrow with my sister. We're shopping for our dresses.'

And then she said hesitantly, 'I never said thank you for making sure Delphi's wedding could be organised so quickly.'

Leo's face was cast in shadow, so Angel couldn't see his expression, and all he said was 'It was part of our agreement, remember?'

Angel's mouth felt numb. 'Of course.' And she turned and went into her bedroom.

Leo knew he should be making his calls—they were important, and an entire boardroom was in New York right now, waiting for him to contact them—but…he couldn't get Angel's face out of his head. And the dark shadows of tiredness he'd seen under her eyes. He couldn't get the roller coaster of the past days and nights out of his head, when everything as he knew it had been turned upside down and inside out. When only one thing seemed to make sense: Angel Kassianides in his bed.

It was as if the fog and haze that had clouded his brain since he'd caught Angel in the study was clearing slightly, and the extent to which he'd become consumed by her shocked him. The anatomy of their relationship was so utterly different from any other he'd known. And he still couldn't get a handle on Angel. She was an enigma. A dangerous enigma.

He couldn't get out of his head the way she'd just thanked him for organising her sister's wedding. When she had been so quick to jump on it and use it as a bargaining tool—no doubt ensuring her own future as well as her sister's. There had been something about it that niggled at him now.

Leo knew that she'd had plenty of opportunity to speak with her father, and yet she hadn't. On the few occasions she'd gone out it had been to meet her sister. She'd gone nowhere near her own home. So that pointed to her father not being involved. But Leo knew he would be a fool to let go his suspicions entirely.

One thing he knew: the more time he spent with Angel, in bed or out, the less logical he became.

Maybe it was time to start pulling back, getting some perspective on things.

He finally picked up the phone, and spent the next couple of hours doing his best to forget all about the woman asleep upstairs.

A week later Angel lay in bed. Alone. It was late. Leo had rung earlier to say that he had to work late and that she should eat at home. It wasn't the first night in the past week that this had happened, and, rather than making Angel feel relieved at having a reprieve of sorts, it made her feel slightly nervous.

Leo had been so all-encompassing, so passionate since the moment they'd met, that it was a shock to see this more distant side to him. She heard a noise then: the unmistakable sound of Leo moving around his room. She held her breath, but as the minutes ticked by he didn't come in.

Angel turned over and stared into the dark. She hated the fact that she couldn't feel relieved he wasn't coming in. Hated the fact that her body throbbed with need. She closed her eyes, but opened them again quickly when lurid images filled her mind. She'd never thought that sex could be so...so... *exciting*. And addictive. She felt like some kind of sex addict; the minute she saw Leo her hormones seemed to go into overdrive and she had zero will-power when it came to resisting him. He only had to look at her and she caught on fire.

Angel couldn't help but suspect that this had to be part of his plan of revenge. After all, he was so much more experienced than her.

She tried her best to sleep, but even after everything had gone silent next door sleep still eluded her, so she gave up and sat up, swinging her legs out of bed. She'd get some water from the kitchen…

Padding down through the quiet villa, Angel felt a jolt, thinking back to the party that night, all those weeks before. Never in a million years would she have imagined that she'd be here, ensconced as Leo Parnassus' mistress.

Too late, just as she was pushing open the kitchen door, she realised that she wasn't the only night visitor. Leo sat at the island in the middle of the kitchen, illuminated under a circle of low light from overhead. He looked up as she came in. He was eating something. Angel instinctively started backing away, feeling as if she was intruding on a private moment. 'Sorry. I didn't realise you were up.'

Leo waved a hand, gesturing for her to come in. 'You couldn't sleep?'

Angel hovered awkwardly and shook her head, 'No.' She felt self-conscious in loose pyjama bottoms and a skimpily clinging vest top, but knew it was silly to feel self conscious when this man seemed to know more about her own body than she did. Not that he seemed inclined to be all that interested any more. Insecurity lanced her. 'I just wanted to get some water.'

It would be ridiculous if she left now, so she went to the fridge in the corner and busied herself getting out a bottle, trying to ignore the way her pulse had rocketed. She hated to think that he might see something of how much she craved him.

Out of the corner of her eye she saw that Leo was wearing a T-shirt and jeans. Angel glanced at him surreptitiously. He might have been working late in the study after he'd come home. She noticed that he had faint smudges of colour under his eyes and felt a spike of concern. Something else caught her eye then, distracting her. Despite herself she moved closer to where Leo sat at the gleaming counter, clutching the bottle of water to her chest.

'Is that peanut butter and *jam*?'

Leo nodded and finished eating a mouthful of sandwich. Angel must have looked bemused, because Leo wiped his mouth with a napkin and said dryly, 'What?'

She shook her head and moved closer to the stool opposite Leo, unconsciously resting against it for a moment. 'I just…I wouldn't have expected…' she said inanely, feeling like a

complete idiot. But there was just something so
disarming about finding Leo like this that her
stomach had turned to mush. Without realising
what she was doing, she sat on the stool opposite him.

'Want one?' he offered, with a quirk of his mouth.

Angel shook her head, slightly transfixed.

Leo started putting lids back on the jars. 'My
ya ya was the one who introduced me to it. She
used to say that peanut butter and Jell-O was the
only thing that made living in the States bearable.
We'd sneak down to the kitchen at night, and she'd
make sandwiches and tell me all about Greece.'

Angel felt a strange ache in her chest. 'Sounds
like she was a lovely lady.'

'She was. And strong. She gave birth to my
youngest uncle when they were a day away from
Ellis Island on the boat from Greece. They both
nearly died.'

Angel didn't know what to say. The ache grew
bigger. She started hesitantly, 'I was close to my
ya ya too. But she didn't live with us. Father and
she didn't get on, so she only visited infrequently.
But as we grew up Delphi, Damia and I would go
and see her as much as we could. She taught us
all about plants and herbs…cooking traditional
Greek dishes—everything Irini, my stepmother,
wasn't interested in.'

Leo frowned. 'Damia?'

'Damia was our sister. Delphi's twin.' Familiar pain lanced Angel.

'Was?'

She nodded. 'She died when she was fifteen, in a car accident on one of the roads down into Athens from the hills.' Angel grimaced. 'She was a bit wild, going through a rebellious phase. And I wasn't here to…' She stopped. Why was she blathering about all of this now? Leo wouldn't be remotely interested in her life story.

But nevertheless he asked, 'Why weren't you here?'

Angel sent him a quick look. He seemed genuinely interested, and there was something very easy about talking to him like this. She decided to trust it. 'Father sent me to a boarding school in the west of Ireland from the time I was twelve until I finished my schooling, so I could learn about the Irish part of my heritage and see my mother.' Angel conveniently left out the part about how her father had basically wanted her gone.

She looked down for a moment, picking at the label on her bottle of water. 'The worst bit was leaving the girls and *ya ya*. She died my first term there. It was too far for me to come home in time for the funeral.'

Angel looked up again, and pushed down the

emotion threatening to rise when she thought of how she'd not been allowed home for Damia's funeral either—hence Delphi's subsequent clinginess and their intense connection.

Leo just sat there, arms relaxed, and then asked quietly, 'Why did your mother leave?'

Immediately Angel bristled. She never talked about her mother to anyone. Not even Delphi. She felt so many conflicting emotions, and yet Leo wasn't being pushy. Wasn't cajoling. They were making bizarre late-night conversation. So with a deep breath Angel told him. 'She left when I was two. She was a beautiful model from Dublin, and I think she found the reality of being married to a Greek man and living a domestic life in Athens too much for her.'

'She didn't take you with her?'

Angel fought against flinching. She shook her head. 'No. I think the reality of a small toddler was also too much for her to bear. She went home, and back to her glamorous jet-setting life. I saw her a couple of times while I was at school in the west of Ireland…but that was it.'

It sounded so pathetic now that Angel told it. Her own mother hadn't deemed her worth keeping. If it hadn't been for the birth of the twins, their instantaneous bond, Angel didn't know how she would have coped.

Leo, seemingly not content with that, asked, 'What was the school like?'

Angel had the strangest sensation of the earth shifting beneath her feet. She quirked a small smile. 'It's in Connemara, one of the most stunning parts of Ireland, but very remote. It's an old abbey, and it looms across a choppy lake like something out of a Gothic nightmare fantasy. When I went that first September it was raining and grey, and it was just…' Angel couldn't help a shudder running through her.

'A million miles from here?'

Angel nodded, surprised that Leo seemed to understand. 'Yes.'

Silence fell, and Angel felt awkward. She'd just told Leo more than she'd ever willingly shared with another person. When he got up to put away the jam and peanut butter she felt a question of her own bubbling up inside her. It was something her father had mentioned that fateful night she'd found him with the will. Afraid to ask, but emboldened after what she'd shared with him, as he came back she said, 'What happened to your mother?'

Leo stopped in his tracks and put his hands on his hips. The temperature in the air around them dropped a few degrees. But Angel was determined not to be intimidated; she was only asking him what he'd asked her.

'Why do you ask?' he said sharply.

Angel gulped. She couldn't lie. 'Is it true that she committed suicide?'

Leo went even more still. 'And where did you pick up that nugget of information?'

Angel had to say it, even though she knew that it would damn her to hell for ever in his eyes. 'The will.'

His body had gone taut, his eyes to obsidian black. No gold. He seemed distant, as if he wasn't even really aware that Angel was there any more. And then he laughed curtly. 'The will. Of course. How could I have forgotten? Yes, I do believe that my mother's suicide is mentioned there—while omitting the gory details, of course.'

Angel wanted to put out a hand and tell Leo to stop; he was looking at her but not *seeing her.*

'I saw her. Everyone thinks to this day that I didn't see her, but I did. She'd hung herself with a torn sheet from one of the banister railings at the top of the stairs.'

Horror and sorrow filled Angel's heart. But instinctively she kept quiet.

'My parents' marriage was an arranged one. The only problem was that my mother loved my father, but he loved building up the business and reclaiming our home in Greece more than her—or me. My mother couldn't cope with being sidelined, so she got more and more manipulative, more and more extreme in trying to get his attention. She started with emotional outbursts, but that just turned my father in on himself. The more tears, the less he'd react. Then she started self-harming and claiming that she'd been mugged. When that didn't work, she took the ultimate step.'

Angel had gone cold inside. What a hideous, hideous thing to have borne. She knew from reading between his words that Leo had seen a lot more than anyone had believed. Not just the suicide. She remembered his reaction to seeing that couple arguing in public, how disgusted he'd looked.

She stood up from the stool. 'Leo, I…' She shook her head. What could she say that wasn't going to sound inept, ridiculous?

Leo finally looked at her properly, as if coming to, and a shiver went down Angel's spine. She'd no doubt that he'd resent having told her this.

'"Leo, I…" *what*?' he asked, his voice harsh.

Angel stood tall. She knew that he hurt, but it wasn't her fault. 'There's nothing I can say that won't sound like a worthless platitude…except that I'm sorry you went through that. No child should have to see something so awful.'

Angel's lack of crocodile tears and her simple yet sincere-sounding statement did something to Leo. It broke something apart inside him. He felt a nameless emotion welling upwards, and knew the only way to push it down would be to find release. A release he'd been denying himself in the belief that he was regaining control, when control was the last thing he seemed to have in his possession.

He was done with denying himself what he wanted and what he needed. But damned if he was going to let Angel know how badly he needed her. She was going to admit her hunger for *him*.

CHAPTER EIGHT

LEO was looking at her so intensely that Angel quivered. And then he just said, in a hard voice, 'We're not here to chat and swap life stories, Angel, charming as this has been. I'm done with talking. What I'd like right now is for you to show me what you've learnt and seduce me.'

Angel just looked at him, hurt slicing through her at the way he was dismissing what they'd just shared and closing himself off again. She could deduce that he wanted to punish her in some way for having encouraged him to talk, but for her to seduce *him*? Show him what she'd learnt? She still had no idea what she was doing in bed—no conscious thought anyway. The minute Leo touched her she forgot time and space, everything but the building fire in her body, and now he wanted…

He said it again, as if he could hear her inner dialogue. 'I want you to seduce me. You're my mistress, that's what mistresses do.'

More hurt sliced through Angel. She was his mistress, and she'd forgotten for a tiny moment. The last days when he'd not come to her bed had left her feeling on edge. She hated to admit it now, especially when he was being so cold, but a part of her *thrilled* at the thought of being free to touch Leo any way she wished.

She told herself that when he pushed her back like this it should make it easier to cut out her emotions…but she caught his eyes and in a flash something glimmered in their depths. Something indefinable. She didn't believe it for a second, but Leo looked almost vulnerable. It made her make her mind up. Along with the way her pulse had jumped to think he was inviting her to take the initiative.

She put the bottle of water down on the island behind her and then turned back. She stepped up to Leo and stood in front of him for a long moment. He was so much taller than her, and so broad that she could see nothing behind him.

From here she looked up, to see Leo looking down from under hooded lids. He wasn't moving a muscle. But Angel could see the golden lights in his eyes again, and curiously that comforted her. She brought her hands to his chest and took a deep breath, spreading them out, moving them up over his pectorals, which she could feel under the material of his soft T-shirt.

She moved her hands under the collar of his
T-shirt and on tiptoe, spread them out and
around his neck. She tried to bring his head
down to her level, so she could kiss him, but he
wasn't budging. Angel bit back a retort. Deter-
mination fired her blood: he wasn't going to
make this easy.

She manoeuvred him over to the stool, pushing
him down onto it so he was more on her level, and
she thought she caught a glint in his eye but
couldn't be sure. His feet were on the ground, the
height of the stool no hindrance to him.

Angel moved his legs apart with her body and
stepped right up between them. She stopped for a
minute and looked at the scar above his mouth. She
put out a finger and traced it, before bending forward
and pressing her lips there, above his top lip.

He still wasn't moving. Just looking at her as
dispassionately as if she were speaking Chinese
in a tedious lecture. For an excruciating moment
uncertainty rose up within Angel and she had a
flash of all the women he had been with. All those
blonde scary-looking women who would no
doubt know exactly what to do, who'd be bringing
him to the edge of his control already, not leaving
him looking as if he was about to fall asleep.

Angel stopped, and her hands fell to his thighs.
She felt stupid. Kissing his scar as if she could kiss

away whatever had put it there. She hung her head. 'Leo, I don't think I can do—'

'Keep going.' His voice was rough.

She looked up again. Leo's eyes weren't as clear as she'd thought. They burned gold. Angel's heart started to thump erratically. Her hands were still on his thighs and she started to move them experimentally up his legs, until they rested near his crotch. Her thumbs were close to where the fabric of his jeans was slightly bulging out.

Angel looked at Leo and moved one hand, so that it cupped him intimately. To her intense joy she could feel the evidence of his arousal and see the way his eyes flared. It gave her a heady confidence. She moved her hand up and down, stroking, caressing through the material. She could see Leo's fists clench out of the corner of her eye, and he made a slight move. Immediately she moved back out from between his legs and away.

She shook her head. 'No touching.'

Leo's jaw clenched, but he nodded. Angel moved back and placed her hand on him again. He was even bigger now, and she started to tingle all over, anticipation coiling through her like a live wire.

With one hand on him, and the other around his neck, she leant into him fully and pressed her mouth to his. In keeping with his letting her do the work, Leo didn't respond to the kiss at first. Angel had to entice and cajole. At one stage she nearly screamed her frustration; despite his obvious arousal, she felt as if *she* was on the way to exploding, not him.

Her breasts were pressed against his chest, and the tips ached so badly that she rubbed against him. She wanted to press herself against his erection, to feel the slide of it against her body.

But his mouth... first she had to get him to kiss her. She flicked out her tongue and traced lightly along the seam of his lips, biting gently and then smoothing over the bites. When she tugged on his lower lip he opened them slightly, and Angel brought both hands to his head, holding him so that she could plunder and stroke her tongue against his exactly the way he did to her. His tongue duelled with hers, teeth nipping, biting her lower lip, making it sting deliciously.

She was in danger of being sucked down into the familiar pool of pleasure—until she noticed that Leo was still restraining himself, even though he was kissing her back. Although when she pulled back slightly she could see a slight sheen of sweat on his forehead. It helped her regain her composure. She tried to control her breathing, stood back and held out her hand. Leo took it and stood up, and Angel silently led him from the kitchen and up the stairs to his bedroom.

It was all at once incredibly intimidating and incredibly arousing to have Leo just say nothing, be passive. When his bedroom door closed behind them Angel turned to Leo and tugged the bottom of his T-shirt up. He lifted his arms and Angel pulled it off all the way.

Then she led him over to the bed and sat him down on the edge. She stepped back a few paces and bit her lip for a second, feeling nervous again. She reached up and pulled at the band that was holding her hair up haphazardly, and felt the mass fall down around her shoulders.

Then she put her hands to the bottom of her flimsy vest and pulled it up slowly, more out of intense nervousness than an attempt to be erotic. She could see a muscle pop in Leo's jaw, and his eyes had darkened. As he lounged back he put his hands behind him in an utterly nonchalant yet effortlessly sexy pose.

For a second Angel's eyes fell to his crotch and she saw the distinctive bulge. Her throat went dry, and she realised she'd stalled, baring her belly. With a deep breath she pulled her vest up and off completely, trying not to feel embarrassed. She let it drop to the ground. Her breasts felt tight and achy, the tips puckering under Leo's hot gaze.

Angel brought her hands to her pyjama bottoms and she undid the tiny bow holding them up. She pulled it loose and the bottoms sagged around her hips. With a little wiggle, she let them fall off.

Angel stepped out of them, and now she stood before Leo in nothing but her tiny panties. He filled her vision. He was like a marauding pirate, inspecting her for his delectation.

Angel walked over to him and pushed his legs apart, coming between them. She brought her hands to the fastening of his jeans and undid the button, slowly dragged down the zip. Her eyes followed the dark silky line of hair that disappeared under the top of his briefs. She saw him wince as her knuckles brushed his erection.

When his jeans were open she put her hands around his back to encourage him to tip his hips up so she could slide them down. Her sensitised breasts brushed enticingly against his belly, and Angel nearly moaned out loud before sinking to her knees to pull them off completely.

With shaking hands, she threw them behind her. She reached up again and tugged at the sides of his briefs. Leo's face was tense, the lines stark. His eyes glittered, and Angel wasn't sure how she was still operating.

She pulled his boxers down, releasing him from confinement. And then, with her heart nearly leaping out of her throat, she looked at Leo and took him in her hand, slowly slipping it up and down over the thickness, feeling him swell and harden even more.

Acting on instinct, wanting to taste every bit of him, she leant forward. But Leo stopped her, with his voice sounding tight. 'No, Angel, you don't have to—'

'No talking.' Her voice was husky and wound around his every sense, pulling tight. Leo couldn't believe it. Angel was shielding those incredible blue eyes by lowering her lashes and taking him into her mouth, surrounding him with sweet, moist warmth. Caressing him with such innocent eroticism that he knew he wouldn't last—not when he'd nearly exploded just at the touch of her hand on him through his jeans downstairs.

Seeing her take off her clothes just now—first that skimpy vest which had shown all too readily the curve of her firm breasts with their hard tips, then the way she'd dropped her bottoms to the floor and stepped out of them. And then she had walked towards him and stripped *him*. He'd actually been afraid to touch her, afraid he'd scare her with the strength of the passion running through him, but he knew she'd pushed him to the edge now, and he wouldn't be able to contain it any longer.

Angel felt Leo's hips jerk, and then suddenly she was being gently pulled away and he was hauling her up.

'Enough,' he growled. 'I'm seduced.' With quick hands he tugged and pulled down her panties, and then, in a move so fast he made her dizzy, she was flat on her back on the bed and Leo was rolling a condom onto his penis.

He pushed her legs apart with a hand, stroking up her thigh as he did so, delving into where the ache was building to screaming pitch. She nearly bucked off the bed she was so aroused. Leo slid into her and then thrust harder and harder, taking her with him, putting a hand under her buttocks, lifting her into him even more. Angel wrapped a leg around his back and clung on. She couldn't breathe, couldn't think, could only move in tandem with Leo until everything was obliterated and shattered around them.

The next morning when Angel woke she was on her front, with one leg lifted up and her arms sprawled out wide. She felt utterly replete at a very deep level, and heavy—as if she could sink all the way to Middle Earth.

She heard a muted sound, and opened one eye to see Leo standing at the mirror of his wardrobe, knotting his tie. It was the same image as that first morning, and she was awake instantly, pulling a sheet over her nakedness, coming up on one arm, wary. She hadn't woken in his bed before.

Leo looked at her, and Angel steeled herself. 'You're still here. And I'm in your bed.'

Leo's mouth quirked and his attention went back to his tie. 'You're very good at stating the obvious.'

Angel bit her lip when she remembered last night. The conflagration that had blown up around them. What had led up to it.

'Do you ever wake up with a woman you've slept with?' she heard herself asking, as if someone had taken control of her mouth.

Leo's hands stilled. Angel could see that the glimmer of warmth in his eyes was rapidly cooling.

Leo tried not to look at Angel, but he didn't have to. Her image was burned onto his retina. She lay there, just feet away, in such tousled and innocently sexy splendour that she hit him right between the eyes. But her question… The very impertinence of it went through him like a gunshot. His immediate reaction had been a vociferous *no*! Because waking up with a woman in his arms was anathema to him on so many levels.

It implied a level of trust he just did not have. For him, trust meant emotion, and emotion meant instability, *fear, and, quite literally, death*. His primary female role model, his mother, had been dangerously unstable. He'd only told Angel the half of it last night—and why the hell had he said anything?

Irritation snaked through him now. He'd come

ABBY GREEN   191

dangerously close to waking up wrapped around
Angel like a vine as it was. With her body curled
trustingly into his. And that was bad enough.

Angel knew Leo wouldn't answer her. She
couldn't believe she'd asked the question. She sat
up and wrapped the sheet around her as she got
up to look for her discarded clothes, blushing
when she bent down to pick up her knickers from
where Leo had flung them in his haste last night.

She was almost at her own door when she
heard his cool, 'We're going out tonight. I'll be
home by eight.'

Angel stopped and just nodded her head,
keeping her back to him. She couldn't bear to see
that same image again, those cool eyes in the
mirror. She slipped into her room and shut the
door behind her.

Back to square one. Back in her place. Delphi's
wedding was only a week away now. Perhaps Leo
saw that as the end of Angel's penance and he'd
turn around the morning after and let her go. He'd
replace all the beautiful clothes in the walk-in
wardrobe with a different size for a new and
improved mistress. One who didn't come with
messy ties and revenge.

Angel resolutely went straight into her shower
and stood under steaming hot jets of water. At
least she had something to look forward to apart

from Delphi's wedding: her jewellery commission for Ari and Lucy Levakis. Just thinking of that and anticipating what she'd start with that day helped to clear her mind of far too disturbing thoughts, like how disarming it had been to see a totally different side to Leo last night.

The day of Delphi's wedding dawned, and Angel was getting ready at the villa. She'd agreed with Delphi that it would be best to avoid her father at all costs. At least they were fairly certain he'd not make a scene at the church, would be too conscious of his peers watching his every move. Leo had gone to the office and was going to go to the church separately, as Angel would be preoccupied with Delphi.

Butterflies erupted in Angel's chest. This was it. The culmination of what she'd agreed with Leo that night just over a month ago. To become his mistress in exchange for arranging Delphi's wedding. Why was she feeling butterflies of trepidation? Because this could be it? Here alone in her room she had to admit that she wasn't prepared for this to be it, no matter how masochistic she knew that made her. It would be Leo's ultimate revenge. Reel Angel in, show her a taste of paradise and then discard her like trash.

And Angel knew well that the paradise she

spoke of had nothing to do with the 'luxuries'
Leo no doubt expected she enjoyed. It was a
paradise of another kind: the paradise of
becoming a woman, of discovering her sensuality.
The paradise of such exquisite lovemaking that
Angel knew no other man would ever have the
same effect on her.

She looked at herself in the mirror. Big blue
eyes stared back at her, shining, glittering. Her
cheeks were flushed.

Since that night in the kitchen nearly a week
ago Angel had been battling her feelings. Trying
to tell herself that what she felt was only akin to
a victim falling for their kidnapper. She frowned.
There was a name for that condition…*yes, love*,
crowed a little mocking voice.

Angel paled visibly in the mirror. How could she
possibly have fallen in love with Leo Parnassus,
when he'd shown her nothing but cold calculation?
Because, she reasoned, he'd been perfectly justified
in believing that she'd come to steal from him. *She*
wouldn't have believed her either. Not with all the
history that lay between their families. It was perfectly conceivable that Angel had been out to try
and save her family by any means possible. And yet
Leo had kept so admirably to his side of the
equation that any minute now a car was coming to
pick her up to bring her to the church where her

pregnant sister would get married to her childhood sweetheart and all would be well for them.

And that was all that mattered, right? Even without all the obstacles between Angel and Leo, there could be no future. The man wasn't even used to sharing a whole night with a woman in his bed, never mind his life…

A sound came from Angel's bedroom door and she turned, expecting to see Calista to tell her the car had arrived. But it was Leo, stunning in a steel-grey suit, white shirt and tie.

Angel's heart tripped; her hands went clammy. 'What are you doing here?'

Leo mocked, 'So pleased to see me? I must surprise you more often.'

Angel blushed fiercely. She knew what had just been going through her mind, and here he was, *unsettling her*, or… Her heart stopped. Perhaps he was here to tell her—

'I thought I'd come for you myself, that's all. You'd better get a move on.'

Angel broke out of the stasis she was in and quickly checked her reflection again, seriously flustered now. Her bridesmaid's dress was a dark dusky pink, strapless and to the knee. Her hair was up in a chignon and she wore a flower in her hair the same colour as the dress.

Grabbing her wrap, she tottered out unsteadily

in high heels, hoping that Leo hadn't seen anything of the naked emotions on her face before she'd hidden them.

Angel thankfully managed to have as little to do with her father as possible during the wedding, but she felt his malevolent stare on her periodically. When she watched Stavros and Delphi walk around the altar three times, with the stefana crowns on their heads, she had to fight back tears, feeling inordinately weepy. She studiously avoided Leo's eye throughout the ceremony, terrified again that he'd see her emotions bubbling so close to the surface. For she who had a somewhat jaded view of marriage to be so moved had scared her slightly.

Before they left for the reception Stavros took her aside and told her how thankful he and Delphi were to her, for helping their wedding to happen, and especially before the pregnancy became common knowledge. Those words alone, and seeing the unmitigated joy on Delphi's face, made everything worthwhile.

Leo was waiting for her at the entrance of the church, to take her to the reception, and to her relief her father didn't seem to be inclined to make a scene—no doubt very well aware that Leo was being courted and feted by everyone almost as if *he* was the one getting married.

Dimitri Stephanides, Stavros's father, had put on a lavish display in a top Athens hotel—no doubt also to impress Leo. Everyone was there. Angel became slowly aware that things had changed subtly in the time that she'd been with Leo. There were fewer of the snide whispers and furtive looks, and the headlines in the newspapers had all but disappeared. She realised that people had grown used to seeing them together…

'Dance?'

Angel looked up from her preoccupation to see Leo standing there, holding out a hand. She stood up and let him lead her to the dance floor, where Delphi and Stavros had just had their first dance to much raucous applause.

A slow, swoony song came on and Leo pulled Angel close. Feeling raw, she tried to resist the pull to just lean against him, but his hand on her bare back, above the top of her dress, urged her close. She gave in and moved and swayed with Leo, content to let her head fall into his shoulder. It felt like sheer indulgence.

'Your sister is not what I expected.'

Angel tensed, but Leo's hand on her back, moving in slow, sensual circles, forced her to relax again. She lifted her head and looked up. Leo's face was far too close for comfort.

'What do you mean?' she asked, half forgetting what he'd said.

He shrugged minutely, one broad shoulder moving under his shirt. He'd taken off his jacket and tie, so his shirt was open to reveal the strong, bronzed column of his throat.

'She seems...' Leo grimaced. 'Sweet. If I didn't know better, I'd say that she and Stavros are genuinely in love.'

Angel really tensed then, and tried to pull away, but Leo was like a steel wall around her, not letting her go anywhere.

She whispered up at him fiercely, 'They *are* in love, and have been for ever. They were childhood sweethearts.'

'Cute,' Leo said, clearly not impressed.

Angel hesitated, and then said in a rush, 'The reason they needed to get married so quickly is because Delphi is nearly four months pregnant. Stavros's family were never going to sanction a marriage with a Kassianides. Stavros wanted to elope with Delphi, but she wouldn't let him do that.'

Leo quirked a brow. Angel bit her lip. She'd gone too far now to turn back.

'His family would have disinherited him and cut him off.'

Angel saw the cynical gleam come into Leo's eye and colour bloomed in her cheeks as she asserted passionately, 'It's not like that. Delphi couldn't care less about Stavros's inheritance, but he wants to get into politics and she didn't want to be responsible for causing a rift in his family.'

'And yet now, no matter what you say, she— and you by proxy—will be fine, secure in the wealth of her new husband.'

Angel finally managed to pull away from Leo with a violent tug, disappointed at how hurt she was at this evidence of his bitter cynicism. 'Believe what you want, Leo. Someone like you will never know that kind of pure love.'

And before he could grab her back she'd spun on her spindly heels and was threading through the couples on the dance floor and out to the lobby. Leo raked a hand through his hair, aware of eyes on him. Aware of the way females were starting to circle, sensing an opening. Beyond irritated, and not even sure why, he pushed through the crowd and went to the bar—but not before he glanced to his right and saw the happy couple.

They were sitting apart from everyone else, in a corner, smiling. Stavros had his hand on Delphi's belly and her hand was over his, and they shared a look of such private intensity that Leo's step almost faltered. Right now they looked nothing like what he'd just described; he felt guilty—as if he'd tarnished something.

Delphi was like Angel only in height and build; the younger sister had obviously inherited her father's stronger features and dark eyes, while Angel must have inherited her Irish mother's more delicate features and colouring.

Leo thought then of what it must have been like to lose their sister, Delphi's twin... At that moment he saw Ari and Lucy Levakis approach and smile a greeting, and for once he was glad of the distraction. Seeing Angel's family was throwing up far too many contradictions.

When Angel felt composed enough she came back into the ballroom, and was surprised to see Leo dancing a traditional Greek dance with the rest of the men. She was still burningly angry with him, but she melted inside when she saw the wide grin on his face. He looked so powerfully sensual doing the dance movements that she couldn't help smile. Just then her arm was grabbed in a punishing grip, and she let out a gasp of pain. *Her father.*

'We need to have a little chat. I've missed you, daughter, and you've been very busy since I saw you last.'

Alcohol fumes wafted over Angel, making her feel sick. She tried to wrench her arm away but her father held on. 'No, we don't. There was no way I was going to let you get away with stealing that man's will.'

Her father sneered. 'So you ran straight to lover-boy and handed it back. Don't think you're going to get away with this, Angel, I'm not finished with—'

Just then Delphi came up and pulled her away. Angel sent her sister a relieved glance as they left their father swaying drunkenly, looking after them murderously. Now that Delphi would be living with Stavros Angel knew she'd never have to see her father again if she didn't want to. The relief was immense, and she gave Delphi a quick, impetuous kiss.

It was the turn of the women now, and the men sat and watched as they all lined up and danced. Angel had taken off her shoes, and was laughing as she bumped into Delphi. She caught Leo's eyes as he watched from the sidelines. She found she couldn't look away, the intensity on his face holding her captive as she made the steps that she knew by heart. That every Greek person knew by heart.

It felt like the most primitive of mating rituals. When the music died away and the DJ started again, Delphi whispered to Angel, saying cheekily, 'If those looks are anything to go by, Leo won't be letting you wait around to say goodbye…'

Angel knew her sister was heading off on honeymoon the next day, so she wouldn't see her for at least a few weeks. She felt very bereft after looking out for her for so long. She also felt uncharacteristically sad for herself; her mother had abandoned her at such an early age, her father had always resented her, and any day now Leo would be turning around and telling her he'd had enough. She felt a little like a piece of flotsam and jetsam, about to be rushed downstream by an oncoming current.

But Leo was standing in front of her. She saw he was holding his jacket. 'Ready to go?'

Angel nodded, feeling incredibly weary all of a sudden. She did not want another run-in with her father, so she got her shoes and let Leo take her hand to lead her out.

Two days after the wedding Leo walked into the villa and, after putting his briefcase in the study, strode across the hall, heading for the room Angel used as a workshop. Anticipation was fizzing in his blood. He'd come home early the day before and stood watching her for a long time before she'd noticed his presence.

Once again he'd found himself reacting helplessly to her, his eyes devouring her slim figure in a white vest and battered loose dungarees folded at the waist. Intent on her task, with her hair in a high knot and big protective glasses on, she shouldn't have been so alluring, but she had been. The fact that his control around her was as woeful as ever had made him feel vulnerable.

All sorts of contradictory feelings were running through Leo now. He'd seen her talking to her father at the wedding; well, to be more accurate, he'd seen her father talking to her, and it had looked extremely intense. It had made him suspect that perhaps they'd known that that would be their only chance to meet, hence the fervour. And then he'd seen her conspiratorial looks and smiles with her sister. No matter that he'd revised his opinion of his sister's motives for getting married, suddenly he doubted himself again.

The facts were still stark: he'd caught her in the act of theft. A detail which seemed to be getting conveniently forgotten far too often. Something hardened inside Leo.

Just then Calista came out of another room nearby. She stopped him in his tracks and asked with a worried look on her face, 'Have you seen Angel?'

He shook his head, feeling irrationally self-conscious. 'No, not yet.'

Calista pointed back to the main part of the house. 'She's in the kitchen.'

Calista bustled off and Leo just stared after her.

What was going on? And what was Angel doing in the kitchen?

Leo strode towards the kitchen, irritation spiking. He found that all the doubts that had begun to assail him had got stronger and stronger. The feeling that perhaps he'd been even more of a monumental fool than he'd thought. Angel and Delphi had got the wedding they'd wanted; he'd taken Angel into his bed. Were she and her father plotting right now to do something— ? He stopped at the kitchen door when he saw Angel at the counter by the sink.

Her back was to him, but there was a set to her shoulders that seemed awfully fragile. She was dressed in a T-shirt and tracksuit bottoms. He glanced at his watch. They were due to go out to a film premiere in less than an hour, but Angel was nowhere near ready. Though he had to concede she got ready more quickly than any woman he'd ever known; she never played silly games and kept him waiting for the grand entrance.

He walked in and saw her shoulders tense. Her hair was down and she didn't turn around. In light of his recent thoughts he felt anger start to bubble down low. He wasn't used to being so sceptical of his decisions. He remembered that night in the kitchen, telling her all about his mother.

It made his voice harsh now as he came round

and saw her profile, saw that she was making some kind of meatballs. That domesticity rankled. 'We're going out this evening.'

Angel didn't turn to look at him; she just said in a quiet voice, 'If you don't mind I'd like to stay in tonight. I'm tired. But you go out.'

Something about her was so intensely vulnerable that it made the hardness swell in Leo's chest. If she thought she was going to start playing games with him now... 'Angel, we have an agreement. Just because your sister got the wedding she wanted it does not mean your job as my mistress is finished.'

Angel flinched minutely, as if stung. She sent Leo a quick glance without really looking at him. 'Look, it's just for this evening. I really am tired.'

Something about the tenseness of her stance struck him then, and the tightness in her voice. *Something was wrong.* Instinctively Leo put out a hand and wrapped it around Angel's arm. She tensed, so rigid that he frowned. 'Angel... what—?'

He had to exert pressure to get her to turn around and face him. He put two hands on her arms now, exasperation lacing his voice. 'Angel, what's got into you?'

She was looking down, hair covering her face. Leo put a finger under her chin and tipped her face up. Something caught his eye, and for a second he couldn't believe what he was seeing. Then something primal exploded out of him. 'What the *hell* is that?'

CHAPTER NINE

ANGEL felt Leo put a hand to her face, tipping it to him slightly, and she closed her eyes. She hadn't wanted him to see her like this; she'd wanted him to just say, 'Okay, fine, I'll go without you.' But he hadn't. She knew what he was looking at: her swollen jaw covered with a livid bruise.

Angel tried to pull free, but Leo wasn't budging. He pushed her hair back behind her ear to have a better look. His voice was grim. 'Have you put ice on this?'

Angel looked into his eyes for the first time. 'It'll hurt.'

Leo shook his head. 'Only for the first few seconds.' And then very gently he probed and felt her jaw. Angel winced and sucked in a breath. Leo swore softly. 'It's not broken, but maybe we should get it checked out at the hospital.'

Angel shook her head. 'No, no hospital. It's just sore.'

Leo looked at her until she couldn't bear it and tore her eyes away. Emotion was welling up from deep down and she was afraid she couldn't contain it. He led her over to a stool and made her sit down, lifting her onto it. Then he went to the fridge and got some ice, wrapping it in a towel. He brought it back and ever so gently laid it against her jaw, soothing Angel when she moved to pull away instinctively. The pain made spots dance before her eyes for a second, and then the coolness was beautifully numbing.

To her abject horror she could feel hot tears welling, and before she could stop them they were overflowing and falling down her cheeks. She gave a dry sob. 'I'm sorry, I just—'

Shock was starting to set in too; she'd been holding it back since it had happened. But now she could feel her teeth start to chatter, her limbs shaking uncontrollably. Leo said something rapid in Greek over her head. Angel dimly guessed it had to be to Calista. Calista who had wanted to ring Leo earlier, but Angel hadn't let her.

In moments Calista was back, and tutting, and handing a glass of what looked like brandy to Leo. Leo dismissed the other woman and made Angel take a sip of the amber liquid. It had an immediate effect. Leo gently wiped at the tears caught on her cheeks.

After a few minutes of letting the drink have its effect, Leo took the ice from Angel and gently led her off the stool and out of the kitchen. He said something else to Calista, who was hovering nearby—something about ringing his PA to tell her he was unavailable for the evening.

He was leading Angel into the informal living room when she started to protest. 'No, you should go out. You have that premiere…'

Leo sat Angel down and brought the ice back up to her face. He looked at her steadily. 'Do you really think I'm going to sit through two hours of American inanity while you're here like this?'

Leo took the ice down, placing it on a nearby tray, and inspected her jaw again. And then his eyes speared hers: *no escape*.

'So, are you going to tell me who punched you in the jaw?'

Angel bit her lip. She couldn't lie. Calista knew anyway, and she'd tell Leo in a second. As if reading her mind, Leo said easily, 'Don't even think of trying to defend whoever did this, Angel.'

Angel could feel the colour draining from her face, and Leo cursed softly again, making her sip more brandy.

Eventually, after a long silence, he just raised a brow. He wasn't budging until she told him. 'I…my father came to visit me today.'

She looked down, shamed by her own father. And shamed by how hurt she was after all these years that his lack of love still had the power to hurt. Leo gently tipped her face up to him again.

'Your father did this?'

Angel nodded. 'He had been drinking. He came to tell me how I'd disrespected our family name. Normally I can avoid him, but…he just caught me unawares. I wasn't fast enough. I never expected him to come here.'

Leo's voice was blistering. 'He's done this *before*?'

Angel nodded, more shame coursing through her. She felt so weak. 'Never this bad, though. When I was smaller he'd lash out at me—he's always resented me for reminding him of the humiliation of my mother deserting him…us. I learnt to avoid him. Just today…' Angel wasn't about to reveal that she'd been preoccupied with defending Leo when her father had lashed out with unexpected accuracy.

A lot of pieces started to fall into place in Leo's head. What he'd seen at the wedding; the fact that Angel had been sent to a remote boarding school. 'That's why you haven't been home once since you came here.'

Angel nodded slowly.

Through a granite-like weight in his chest, Leo

asked, 'He really didn't send you here to the villa, did he? The night of the party or the night I found you in the study?'

Angel shook her head. Her heart had leapt into her mouth and was beating so hard she felt a little faint.

'Why were you here that night, then, Angel?'

'The night of the party was exactly as I told you. I had no idea where we were going and then it was too late. I tried to stay in the kitchen, but my boss sent me upstairs…' She blushed. 'I truly didn't know who you were at the pool, or on the terrace. I'd avoided reading anything about your family coming home. I was too ashamed.'

She stopped. She couldn't believe that Leo was listening to her. She willed him to believe what she said. 'And that next night…I wasn't stealing the will. I was trying to return it.'

Leo frowned. 'Return it?'

'I'd come home from work the previous evening and found my father crowing over it… that's how I knew about your mother. He'd sent some of his goons to steal it. To be honest, I'm not sure how he did it, or even if it had been taken from the villa. I just assumed… And when I could, I took it from him and brought it back, thinking I could just leave it in a drawer, or something.'

She looked away for a second, and then back. 'I felt so bad about your family, what you'd been through, and I didn't want him to be responsible for causing more trouble. But then you came in…'

'And the rest is history,' Leo said without humour. Angel had never seen him look so grim.

He shook his head, his eyes dark with something indefinable. Something that made Angel's heart trip unsteadily. 'Angel, I—'

She spoke quickly. 'Leo, I know exactly how it looked. *I* wouldn't have believed me. That's why I didn't even try and defend myself. I knew there was no point. The whole situation was completely damning.'

'No.' A muscle popped in Leo's jaw. 'Your father had to knock you about before I'd see the truth.'

Angel shook her head. 'Leo, don't, please. I brought this on myself.'

Leo was fierce. 'Not like this, Angel, never like this. If I'd thought for a second that your father was capable of this…' Waves of anger vibrated off Leo.

He touched Angel's cheek and said huskily, 'You must be exhausted.'

Angel nodded. 'I am a little.' But she thought of going to sleep, and all the images waiting to crowd her mind: her father's mottled face, the way his hand had come out of nowhere and stunned her so badly that she'd blacked out for a minute, only to come to and see him rifling through the drawers of the study. Thankfully Calista had had the sense to be nearby, and had called the security guard up from the gate. He'd escorted Angel's father from the villa, but not until Angel had insisted that his pockets be searched. Luckily he hadn't found anything worth stealing.

'But I don't want to go to bed…' Her voice was more fierce than she'd intended, and she saw Leo wince.

'Angel, you must know that I wouldn't expect—'

She covered her hand with his, inordinately touched. 'No, I don't mean that. I just mean I don't really want to go to sleep—not just yet anyway. I don't want to think about… what happened.'

Leo nodded. Within minutes Angel was sitting on a comfortable couch in the TV den, with a blanket over her, while Leo went to get some food from Calista. Then he was back and fussing over Angel like a mother hen, making her take some soup, because it would hurt too much for her to have to chew anything.

It felt as if the most delicate chain of silver stretched between them now, connecting them, and Angel clung onto it greedily.

Leo switched on the TV without asking any more questions, and seemed content to watch inane TV, sensing Angel's need to get lost in something. She let the ribald movie wash over her like a balm, and relished Leo's protective arm around her like a guilty secret.

Angel's body had turned into a dead weight against Leo. He looked down at the glossy head that lay against his chest. The hand so trustingly curled against him. So many questions bubbled up inside him, so much recrimination, and underneath it all a fierce, primal anger. He could still see the livid swelling, and wanted to go and find Tito Kassianides and beat him to a pulp. Leo had to consciously calm himself. His heart-rate was already zooming skywards just when he thought of that man.

But, as if in league with his earlier thoughts, an insidious voice mocked him. What if this was all a set-up? What if this was part of a plan—a ruse to arouse his sympathy, his trust in Angel? Leo felt sick at the thought. It couldn't be. *It couldn't be.* She'd been a virgin, for heaven's sake. His body still thrilled with a deep-seated male satisfaction at knowing that he'd been her only lover.

Too much had fallen into place when Angel had explained everything earlier. Leo was disgusted with himself. Was he so jaded, so cynical after witnessing what he had as a child, that he'd believed someone would go to the lengths that Angel had in order to manipulate him?

Grimly, he knew he didn't have to answer that

question. Leo flicked off the TV and without disturbing Angel stood from the couch, lifting her into his arms. He took her up to his bed and, after settling her, took off his clothes and got in beside her, pulling her close.

Angel woke when the dawn was a faint light coming into the room from outside. She registered that she was in Leo's bed, in her panties and T-shirt. She went hot. He must have taken off her tracksuit bottoms when she'd fallen asleep on him downstairs. She was on her side, and Leo was tucked around her, his arm a heavy weight over her waist, his hand close to cupping her breast. He was naked. Despite everything her blood stirred and her body started to hum.

She had a premonition of Leo waking to find that she was still in his bed, and went to move. She heard a deep growl. 'Stay where you are.'

Angel stopped moving, but couldn't pretend she could sleep again—not when she felt Leo's body hardening and firming against hers, making her want to push her bottom against him in clear provocation. Her breathing had grown short and shallow. She lifted her head minutely, to ease a slight ache, and sucked in a breath when pain shot through her jaw, reminding her all too clearly of yesterday's events.

Instantly Leo moved and hovered over Angel, his jaw dark with stubble. With a gentle hand he turned her face so he could see. His eyes and his low curse told her how bad it looked. It felt as if it had turned into the size of a football.

She winced. 'Is it very bad?'

Leo quirked a wry smile. 'It's a glorious shade of blueish purple, and about as big as my fist.' Then he got serious. 'We're going to the hospital today, Angel, I don't care what you say.'

Angel knew better than to argue. She lay there and looked up at Leo, and felt her chest and heart swell. With the impenetrable wall of mistrust between them gone, she realized that she loved him. She really loved him. Without thinking, she reached up and traced the scar above his lip with a finger. 'How did you get that?'

Leo caught her finger and kissed it. 'I'd like to be able to say that I got it while defending a younger kid from being bullied.'

'You didn't?'

He shook his head mock-mournfully. 'No, I got it when I fell off my training bike onto the sidewalk when I was three.'

Angel's heart lurched, and she fell a little bit more in love. She would have smiled if it hadn't hurt, but Leo was tucking himself around her again and saying, 'Go back to sleep, Angel, you need it.'

Angel felt the waves of tiredness coming over her again and said sleepily, 'Okay, but wake me up and I'll go back to my own bed in a bit…'

Angel didn't see the spasm of pain cross Leo's face. Leo lay awake, staring into the dim morning light for a long time.

Two weeks later Angel looked at the finished set of jewellery for Ari and Lucy. She looked at it but didn't really see it. Experimentally she moved her jaw and touched it gingerly. The swelling had gone down completely, and all that remained of the bruise was a faint yellowish tinge that could be covered by make-up.

Leo had taken Angel to a private clinic the day after it had happened and they'd ruled out a fracture; it was just a very severe bruise. Since that night Leo had been amazingly attentive, eschewing all public engagements to stay at home with Angel despite her protestations. From going out practically every night, now they ate in, and Leo had surprised her one night by dismissing Calista and serving up a delicious home-cooked dinner. He was doing absolutely nothing to help her stop falling deeper and deeper in love with him, and she knew that he would not welcome it.

Clearly Leo was feeling guilty at having mis-judged her, despite her assurances that she had been as much to blame by coming here in the first place. He'd insisted that Angel sleep with him every night, but he'd been careful not to touch her. Last night Angel had turned to him in the bed, frustration clawing through her body. She knew Leo was aroused, she felt it every night, but he was making the same protestations. Treating her as if she was made out of china and might break.

Angel had put her hand around him intimately and said, 'I'm better, Leo, *please…*' She cringed now to think of it, of how ardently she'd responded when he'd finally groaned deep in his throat and drawn her on top of him, lifting her vest away, helping her out of her pants. She'd felt as if she'd been starved of water in the desert for a month. But she'd been the one to initiate it, not Leo.

Angel shook her head, and then started violently when she heard a noise come from the door. Leo stood there, nonchalantly leaning against the frame. Her heart turned over as it always did. She smiled shyly. 'Hi.'

Leo smiled too and, slightly mesmerised, Angel thought again that when he smiled he looked a million miles away from the tough tycoon. From the man who had coldly blackmailed her.

He strolled in and looked at Angel's handiwork; she took in his expression nervously, valuing his opinion. He picked up the bracelet and then the earrings, turning them this way and that. Finally he put them down and said, 'You're really good— you do know that?'

Angel half shrugged, embarrassed. 'It's what I love to do, so if I can make a living out of it then I'll be happy.'

Leo put out a hand and trailed a finger gently down her injured jaw. 'It's almost healed.'

Angel nodded. 'I can put some make-up on it for tomorrow night, when we go to Lucy and Ari's for dinner.'

He nodded and then backed away, but for a second Angel could have sworn he'd wanted to say something. She forgot about it, though, when they settled down to eat dinner, after which Leo went into his study to work for a while, and Angel went to her workshop to do some last-minute checks on the jewellery for Lucy. Tomorrow she'd go into town and buy some boxes to package them before they went for dinner.

The following day Leo stood at the window of his office in Athens, looking out at the view, but not registering it. He was consumed with one thing, one person: *Angel*. She was turning him upside down and inside out. For someone who broke out in a rash at the thought of waking up in a bed with a woman, now he couldn't relax properly unless he knew Angel was going to be the first thing he saw every morning.

The guilt of how his behaviour had put her in danger still made him feel nauseous, and yet she'd begged him not to do anything to her father, reminding him that her father would capitalise on the slightest hint of enmity to fuel their feud. The best form of revenge was ignoring Tito, even though it killed Leo to do so.

In the days after she'd been hit it had been easy to restrain himself from touching her sexually. His concern had overridden his desire, and he had also felt something else more disturbing: the knowledge that his making love to Angel had become imbued with something much more ambiguous than revenge. Something that came with silken ties binding around him tightly. Silken ties that reminded him of a time when he'd vowed never to allow someone to get close enough to arouse this awful welling of emotion and feeling.

He shook his head. He hated being introspective, so when his thoughts were cut abruptly short by a soft knock he welcomed it, saying, 'Come in.'

His PA opened the door. 'Ari Levakis is here to see you.'

'Thanks, Thalia, send him in.'

He smiled when he saw Ari walk in, and greeted him heartily. They sat down to discuss the business at hand, neither one needing to stand on ceremony, both trusting each other as only men of a similar standing could.

After an hour of intense discussion Ari sat back with a coffee cup in hand and looked at Leo. Unaccountably Leo felt the hair tighten on the back of his neck.

'I spoke to Angel yesterday. She says she'll have the jewellery ready for this evening when you come to dinner. I hope she hasn't been under too much pressure to get it done.' Ari frowned. 'We haven't seen either of you out lately, so I hope you haven't been slave-driving her.'

Leo smiled tightly and fought the image of coming home every evening that week and finding Angel immersed in her task, covered in the fine dust of the precious metals and stones she'd been working with, dressed in the ubiquitous vest tops and battered dungarees, which always had an instantaneous effect on his arousal levels.

Leo realised he still hadn't answered Ari; he'd got so caught up in his own memory. He flushed, and probably sounded harsher than he'd intended. 'Not at all… We've both been happy to take a break from the social scene. She has been working hard at it, but she's enjoyed doing it.'

That was true. She'd been oblivious to him several evenings, until he'd come in and taken the headphones of her iPod out of her ears, and then she'd turned to him and smiled…

'When I first heard you were seeing her I had my doubts. After all…she is who she is, and she'd turned up like that at your father's house.'

Leo looked at Ari, and something must have shown on his face because Ari spread his hands in a gesture and said, 'What? You can't blame me, Leo. Everyone was thinking the same thing. Athens is full of beautiful women and you went for the most unlikely one—some would have said the most unsuitable one. No one would have blamed you if you'd ignored that whole family in the street.'

Ari only knew the half of it. What would he say if Leo told him what else had happened? Would Ari have jumped to the same conclusion, damning Angel before she'd had a chance to defend herself? Would he have used his knowledge to blackmail her into becoming his mistress? Leo got up, suddenly feeling agitated. Would Angel have ever become his mistress of her own volition?

Leo struggled to articulate some platitude, feeling like a fraud, and not liking his defensiveness. 'Our shared history is our business…there is a certain…synchronicity to how we came together.'

When he said those words Leo had a disturbingly vivid memory of how Angel had felt that first time he'd taken her, how she'd arched beneath him and entreated him to keep going, and how it had taken all of his skill and restraint not to hurt her. Sweat broke out on his brow. He was feeling seriously cornered.

Angel knocked on the outer door of Leo's office. His PA Thalia looked up and smiled warmly. The two had met when Thalia had come to the villa one night to work late with Leo.

'Hi, Angel. He's with Ari Levakis, but they should be done soon. I'm going out for lunch now.' The other woman started to get up from behind her desk, 'He knows I'm going out, but just in case he's forgotten could you remind him I'll be back at two?'

Angel smiled. 'No problem. I just brought him some lunch.'

She watched Thalia leave and then put the small brown paper bag on the desk and walked around the anteroom. It and the whole building screamed wealth and prestige. She'd been on her way home from picking up boxes for the jewellery, and while she was out had decided to make a visit. Angel hadn't been to Leo's office before, and butterflies were beating a symphony in her chest.

She looked at the paper bag and grimaced. She'd bought him a peanut butter and jelly sandwich. Was this the most stupidly transparent thing she'd ever done?

She jumped when the doorknob rattled and the door opened slightly. Leo's meeting must be over. She held her breath, but no one came out. With the door ajar, she could hear the deep rumble of Ari's voice.

'Lucy and I really like her.'

Angel's heart stopped cold, and her breath with it, as she listened. Leo's voice came, deep and strong.

'I know you do.' He said nothing else for a moment, and Angel could imagine him raking a hand through his hair. Even without seeing him she could sense that he was irritated, and wondered why.

'Look, Angel and I…it's just a temporary thing. I have no desire to settle down with the first woman who crosses my path in Athens.'

Ari's voice was dry, and further from the door. He must have moved back into the room. 'I appreciate that she mightn't be the most…*appropriate*…wife material.'

Angel winced, and felt as if a knife were skewering her insides. Leo laughed then, and the knife sank a little deeper.

'Angel becoming a permanent fixture in my life might be taking my father's tolerance levels a little too far, and Athens is still reeling with our association as it is.'

Ari laughed briefly. 'You certainly know how to stir it up, Parnassus…but does Angel know this?'

The temperature in Leo's voice went down a few hundred degrees. 'Angel knows exactly what to expect from this relationship.'

The tone of Ari's voice told Leo that he wasn't intimidated. 'Like I said, Lucy and I really like her. I just hope she *does* know what to expect, we'd hate to see her get hurt…'

A dangerous quality came into Leo's softly spoken words. 'Is that a warning, Levakis?'

Ari was undeterred. 'Take it how you want, Leo… I just don't think Angel is like the other hardened socialites of our circles. Once I might have assumed it, but after getting to know her…'

Leo's voice was hard. 'You don't have to worry. Angel and I know exactly where we stand.'

Ari laughed briefly. 'Lucy sent me here with a flea in my ear…so we'll see you and Angel later. I'm looking forward to seeing the finished pieces.'

Angel didn't wait to hear the rest. On legs that were numb, and feeling as if every ounce of blood had drained from her body, she stumbled back out of the anteroom and all but ran to the lift.

It was only when she was descending that she remembered leaving the brown bag behind. Dread struck her to think that Leo might find it, but she had no intention of going back. She could only stumble out of the lift, into the street, and get away from Leo's office as quickly as she could.

A little later, as Angel polished and finished off the pieces she'd made for Lucy, she bitterly castigated herself. What had she expected, truly…? That Leo had somehow miraculously come to have feelings for her? She was his mistress; he'd taken her because he desired her, because he'd had the power to give Delphi her wedding and because he'd believed Angel guilty of a crime. Since Leo had learnt what had really happened the lines might have got a little blurred for Angel, but after hearing that conversation evidently Leo hadn't felt the same way.

She was the naive fool who had allowed herself to believe that the tenderness he'd displayed in recent weeks had meant something.

Angel's hand went to her belly and she bit her lip. The other night when Angel had all but begged Leo to make love to her they hadn't used contraception. Angel had assured Leo that she was at a safe place in her cycle, but now she wasn't so sure.

The thought that she might get pregnant made her go cold all over—especially after hearing Leo's stark words to Ari today. One thing was crystal-clear: this relationship was heading for closure, and sooner rather than later. Angel knew that Leo would not appreciate being forced into fatherhood by a Kassianides, and what if he thought she'd done it on purpose? She had an awful feeling that he still didn't trust her entirely.

The phone rang then, making her jump, and Angel reached for it. Leo had insisted on getting a phone installed in her workroom.

'Hello?'

'Why didn't you stay?'

Angel's heart tripped, and she gripped the phone with two suddenly slippery hands. *The sandwich*—he must be mortified.

'I…had to get back to package up the pieces. I only dropped in to say hello, but you were busy.'

He said nothing for a moment, and Angel could imagine him sitting in his palatial office.

'Thank you for my lunch.'

Angel laughed, and it sounded false to her ears. 'Oh, God, *that*. I don't know what—'

'It was sweet.'

Angel was glad she was alone, because a raging fire of humiliation was burning her up from her toes to her head.

'I'll be home at seven. See you then.'

And the connection was terminated. Angel's heart was thumping out of control; she felt shaky and clammy all over. She was a mess. She was in love. And she was doomed. The Parnassus family were going to have the last laugh after all.

CHAPTER TEN

THAT evening, after they returned from dinner, Angel felt like a limp rag. For once in her life her joy of making jewellery had been eclipsed by something else, *Leo*, and protecting herself around him. She marvelled at how men could have no feelings invested in a relationship and yet make you feel as if you were the only woman in the world.

All evening Leo had been solicitous. Angel had told herself it was just for show, but when Lucy and Ari had briefly left the room to tend to their children Leo had turned to Angel and taken her face in his hands, pressing a hard kiss to her mouth almost as though he couldn't help it, as though he *needed* it, and her body, traitor that it was, had responded.

It had only been when they'd heard a teasing, 'You know, there are some spare rooms upstairs if you like…' that they'd broken apart. Angel had felt unbelievably raw and shaken.

'Penny for them?'

Angel looked sharply at Leo from where she was taking off her shoes inside the door of the villa. She looked down and shrugged minutely, feeling the intense need to self-protect.

'Nothing, really—just that I hope Lucy likes the earrings and bracelet. It's the first time I've done something in a while and—'

Leo was close, and when Angel stood he tipped her chin up with a finger, making her burn inside.

'She'll love them. Ari loved them. You're extremely talented.'

Angel blushed and could have kicked herself. Why, oh, why couldn't she pull off the whole insouciant thing?

He came too close then, and took her arm just above the elbow. She trembled and tried to pull away. His eyes flashed a little.

'A nightcap?'

Angel answered on instinct, needing to get away, 'Leo, I'm really—'

'Please?'

Something in his face made Angel stop. Her heart beat faster. She shrugged minutely. 'Okay, I guess…'

She followed Leo into the palatial drawing room, a little perplexed. If she didn't know better she'd imagine that he wanted to talk to her about something.

He asked her what she wanted, then poured a

Bailey's for her and a whisky for himself. He handed her the drink.

After a long moment that seemed to stretch taut between them he said, 'Angel, I think we both know that any *arrangement* we had is out of the window. I won't and can't stop you if you want to leave.'

Angel's heart clenched so tight she thought she might faint for a second. Her hands unconsciously clenched around her glass, and she was glad she was sitting down. 'I—' she started to say, but Leo was still talking.

'But I don't want you to go, Angel.'

Her heart started to beat again. 'You don't?' she croaked.

He shook his head. 'We're not finished yet. I still want you.'

We're not finished yet. I still want you. Nothing about love or feelings. But, like earlier, she reminded herself: what did she expect after over-hearing his conversation with Ari?

'The jewellery workspace is yours, Angel—yours for as long as we're together. After this commission from Ari, and with a little advertising, you're going to be inundated with commissions. This could be the start of a real career for you.'

He wasn't even asking her to stay just because she might want to. She couldn't let him see that she was hurting so much inside.

She smiled, but it felt tight. 'So you're saying that if I stay with you, until such time as you or I grow bored, you'll help launch my career? And what if I don't want to stay?'

Leo's eyes turned very black; his jaw tensed. 'I don't think you'll have any problem setting up on your own, Angel, but you can't deny that this is a launching pad that would put you at a whole other level.'

Angel felt sick. What he was doing was so cruel, and yet…he was also handing her the moon, sun and stars. He was right. With patronage from him, her career would be assured. Could she do that, though? Share his bed knowing that some day in the future he'd be letting her go, albeit leaving her with a glittering career as a token prize?

Suddenly all the ambition that Angel had always harboured felt very flat. She knew if she had the choice that she'd take Leo's love over the launching of a successful career. A career could always be pursued—but true love? Clearly love was not a word in his vocabulary, and if he ever did come to settle down it would be with someone eminently more suitable than her.

Angel felt as if she was breaking into little pieces inside, but she took a studied sip of her drink and then looked up. 'Do you know the only reason I didn't leave my home before now?' She laughed briefly. 'No doubt you must have wondered what on earth I was doing there when my father so evidently hated my guts.' She looked away, and then back again. 'I stayed for Delphi. Because after Damia's death she was lost, went in on herself. Irini, her mother, is next to useless, my father is cut off from human emotion…and poor Delphi was there all on her own. So I promised that no matter what I'd stay with her until she was ready to leave. I was hoping after college I'd persuade her to move out with me, but then father's business started to unravel and we just didn't have the money. Delphi's studying law. I worked to help her get through college, but it meant we couldn't leave home.'

Leo was as silent and still as a statue.

'I've been waiting for a long time for my freedom, Leo. Now that Delphi is married to Stavros I can finally go and live my own life.'

Leo's jaw twitched. 'And that's what you want? Despite what I can offer you?'

Angel nodded and forced a brittle smile. 'Getting the commission from Ari is more than I could have ever hoped for in the first place. And I think you must have realised by now that I was never proper mistress material.'

Leo stood tall and dark and dominant. Unmoving. No emotion flickering across his impassive face. Finally he said, 'I have to go to New York tomorrow on business. I'll be gone for about two weeks. I would just ask that you think about what I've said and then decide. I won't push you for a decision now.'

Angel nodded slowly, feeling as though she was being impaled. 'Very well.'

And that was it. Angel got up and put her glass on the drinks board. She turned and said, 'I'm tired. I'm going to bed.'

'Goodnight, Angel.'

And she walked out of the room, knowing that it would be the last time she saw Leo Parnassus.

Leo walked into the villa two weeks later and knew instantly that Angel was gone. He had never, ever faced this prospect: a woman walking away from him. In his supreme arrogance he'd not contemplated that she might go. And yet he hadn't called or made contact because something superstitious had stopped him—almost as if he didn't know, she wouldn't have left. But she had.

He walked to her workspace and opened the door. Everything was cleaned away, all the tools and leftover metals and gems in neat piles and rows. She'd left it all, and a note.

Dear Leo, I've left everything out so that it'll be easy to take away and dismantle. I know it might seem a little weird to say this after everything that happened, and all the circumstances, but thank you for everything. All the best, Angel.

Leo crumpled up the note and stood for a long moment with his head downbent. And then, with an inarticulate roar of rage, he swept an arm along the top of the workbench, sending tools and metals and gems flying. Tiny diamonds winked up at him mockingly from the floor.

Three months later

Angel's lower back ached. She put her two hands there and stretched, arching backwards. She was pregnant, and just beginning to show. The growing thickness of her middle had become a little bump practically overnight. The day after her final conversation with Leo she'd had some spotting, which she'd believed to be her period when in fact it hadn't been. It was only when she'd missed her next period that she'd got worried and had her pregnancy confirmed.

'You should sit down, lovey—take the weight off your feet.'

Angel smiled at Mary, the woman she worked with in the little tourist café in the grounds of the abbey of her old school in the west of Ireland. 'I'm not about to go into labour because of a little lower back pain.'

The older woman, whom Angel had known since she'd started at the school all those years before, when Mary had been the cook there, smiled fondly. 'No. Maybe not. Well, in that case you can see to the latest arrival—some man on his own. I'd say that's it for the day, then. The last tour are pulling out of the car park now.'

Angel picked up her notepad, and a tray to clear off any dirty tables while she was out. She was looking forward to getting back to the tiny house she shared with a niece of Mary's and having a long hot bath. As she walked out into the dining area the evening sun glinted for a moment, so she couldn't see anything.

When she emerged more fully she had the impression of someone tall and dark standing up, a chair scraping back on the floor just before she saw him properly. But she didn't have to see him. She *knew.*

Leo. Tall and imposing and dark and gorgeus. *Leo.*

Angel felt faint. Her blood was draining downwards in a rush and everything tilted alarmingly.

In a second she was in a chair. Leo was crouching down, looking up at her, and Mary was there too, fussing. 'Are you all right, Angela? I knew you shouldn't be on your feet for all that time. Honestly, you're so stubborn.'

Angel had a moment of panic, afraid Mary would say too much, and put out a hand. 'Mary, I'm fine, honestly. I just got a shock, that's all. I know this man…he's an old friend of mine.'

The astute Irishwoman looked from Angel to Leo and summed the whole thing up in an instant. Angel saw the cogs whirring behind the bright blue eyes.

Mary directed her questions at Angel. 'Are you sure you're okay? Do you want me to leave you alone?'

Angel nodded, even though she felt like clinging onto Mary and begging her to stay. She couldn't. She had to face the father of her child.

'I'm fine, Mary, really. You should get home.'

'But what will you do? You've no car, and your bike is at home.'

'I'll take care of her getting home.'

Leo spoke for the first time, and the effect on Angel was nothing short of cataclysmic. Mary left with much huffing and dark looks directed at Leo, but finally they were alone. Leo stood up. He was dressed in jeans and a dark top, dark coat.

Every part of her tingled, as if she'd been frozen numb for a long time and was being brought slowly back to life. She was glad of the voluminous apron, which covered her tiny bump and her secret.

He whirled around then, and those dark flashing golden eyes that haunted her dreams made her breath catch.

'Angela?'

Angel explained, because it was easier than letting her mind implode. 'When I came here to school the nuns didn't think Angel was a suitable name, so they insisted on calling me Angela. Mary worked there, at the abbey, so she calls me Angela too.'

'You have a bike? You cycle to work here on those roads?'

Angel nodded again, noticing that there were lines of strain around Leo's mouth. That couldn't possibly be—

She answered quickly, to stop her mind going down dangerous avenues. Indulgent avenues. 'Yes. I know they're a bit intimidating, but once you're used to them—'

'Intimidating? Those roads are downright suicidal!'

The look on his face, all at once censorious and something else, made Angel stand up. The shock of seeing him here was finally beginning to wear off. How could he come in here and talk about banal things, as if nothing had happened?

'Leo, you're hardly here to discuss the Irish roads. How did you find me?' *Why did you come looking for me?*

He raked a hand through his hair, and Angel noticed that it had grown longer. In fact he looked altogether more dishevelled. He swung away and then back, his eyes intense on hers. 'It took nearly a month of constant badgering to persuade your sister to tell me where you were.'

Angel sat down again, her legs turning to jelly. She'd stayed in Athens for about a month after leaving the villa, and when Leo had made no effort to come after her it had killed something inside her, despite all her best intentions. Despite knowing it was completely irrational to have hoped for that, because she'd left, basically telling him she wasn't interested.

She bit her lip and looked up. 'I…hadn't planned on coming here, but once I found out—' She stopped. It was too bald to just come out with the most monumental thing that had happened to her. She'd always planned on telling Leo she was pregnant with his baby, but once she'd got some distance, got her wits together, and had decided the best way forward. She hadn't expected to face him so soon. But how would he take the news when she'd heard him say what he had to Ari? That conversation was still etched into her brain.

She turned her head away. It hurt to look at him and acknowledge him being here.

Leo came down in front of her and turned her face back to him. There was a tortured expression in his eyes. It made Angel's insides quiver dangerously.

With a sinking feeling Angel knew that now was the time. Distance hadn't healed her hurt or clarified things; it had made it worse.

'Found out what, Angel?'

She felt a delicate fluttering, as if their baby was already siding with its father, demanding she tell the truth.

'I'm pregnant, Leo.'

For a long moment nothing happened. Neither one of them moved. And then Leo did the last thing Angel had expected. She wasn't sure what she'd expected, but it had something to do with a horrorstruck expression or disbelief.

He reached around behind her neck and pulled the apron over her head. Then he pulled her forward and opened the apron at the back. His big hands on her made Angel's pulse quicken, her breathing catch.

'Leo, what are you—?'

But he just stopped for a moment and put a finger to her mouth. 'Shh.'

Then he pulled the apron away, and her bump was bared in all its tiny proud glory, revealed in her figure-hugging black stretchy top. Leo put his hands over it, fingers stretching out around the sides. Angel held her breath, her eyes widening at seeing him like this, prostrate at her feet.

The feel of his hands on her belly was bringing up so many emotions. Angel looked at Leo, and she could see a look of wonder come over his face. She shut down the impulse to indulge in a dangerous fantasy.

'Leo, why did you come here?'

He shook his head, his hands still on her belly. 'How can you ask that? You should have told me, Angel.'

Shame lanced Angel. Leo being disappointed was so much worse than Leo being all arrogant and demanding. She hung her head. 'I didn't know until about two months ago, and then when I found out…'

The moment she'd found out about the pregnancy hormones had taken over, and the thought of bumping into him, or seeing him with a new woman, had been too much to bear. So, like a coward, she'd run to the farthest place she'd known.

Angel lifted her head, feeling some fire come back. She couldn't think with Leo looking at her so closely, touching her. She stood up with effort, dislodging his hands, and stepped away. Instantly she felt bereft.

'Look, Leo, our relationship was never about a happy-ever-after, even if you did want me to stay on as your mistress. I overheard your conversation with Ari Levakis in your office.' Angel waved her hand in agitation, aghast she'd let that slip out so easily. 'What I heard doesn't matter. The thing is, I knew that things would come to an end eventually.'

Her eyes flicked to him, but he looked stonily impenetrable. Angel was so emotional at the moment the smallest thing could set her off. 'Look, Leo, if you've come just to ask me to be your mistress again—'

He crossed his arms and sent a pointed look to her belly. 'I think that we've gone beyond that point now, don't you?'

She reacted from a deep desire to self-protect. 'Leo, I won't have you think that just because I'm pregnant I'm going to submit to some sort of marriage of convenience. I know from what I heard you tell Ari that you'd no plans of settling down with me—I can only imagine how the thought of having to settle down with a Kassianides must turn your—'

'Angel, stop talking.'

Angel stopped. Emotion wasn't far away. Leo's arms dropped and he came closer. Angel would have backed away, but a table was behind her. She put up a hand. 'Leo, please don't…'

'Don't what, Angel? Touch you? I can't help it if we're in the same room. What else? Don't come after you? I can't help that either. I would have gone to the ends of the earth to find you.' His voice was rough.

Angel's heart started beating very rapidly. 'Leo, stop this. Don't think you're going to get the package now, just because you've found me and I'm pregnant and it's all convenient. That's exactly what I don't want.'

Leo seemed to ignore what she'd said, and reached out to loosen the pin holding her hair up. She hadn't had it cut in months and it had grown longer, falling heavily around her shoulders.

'You seem to be doing enough thinking for the both of us.'

He was twining a piece of her hair around his finger, and Angel felt curiously paralysed. He came closer, until she could feel her belly touching him. A fire started down low, preparing her body for him in a way that she hadn't felt for long weeks.

'When you left me, Angel Kassianides, I went to a dark place.'

Angel looked up, mesmerised despite herself. 'You did?'

Leo nodded and grimaced. 'I came home from New York, found your note and you gone. I trashed the jewellery workshop and promptly flew back to New York for a month, where I spent far too much time in a dingy Irish bar.'

He laughed again mirthlessly. 'Then, even though I couldn't even look at another woman, I thought I was over you, I came back to Athens and proceeded to be such an ogre that I made Calista cry, fired countless employees, and currently Ari and Lucy aren't talking to me.'

Angel gasped. 'They're not?'

Leo shook his head, still twirling Angel's hair around his finger. 'It was only after those two torturous months that I finally allowed myself to admit to my hurt that you'd chosen to walk away rather than stay with me. And then I had to convince your sister to tell me where you were.'

Angel took a breath, feeling as if she was stepping into a void. 'But, Leo, you weren't asking me to stay. You were telling me what you'd give me if I'd stay. It was conditional.'

Leo stopped playing with her hair and looked at her properly, and for the first time Angel saw the vulnerability in his eyes. 'I didn't have the guts to ask you to stay just because you wanted to. I was too terrified of you saying no, because I'd never given you a choice in the first place. I thought my only option was to try and force you into it.'

Angel shook her head; something very fragile

was beginning to bloom in her heart. 'To be honest, I probably still would have walked away.' Angel could see the effect of her words on Leo, the tightening and closing of his face, the dimming in his eyes, but before he could retreat into some protective shell completely she took his hand and held it to her breast, under which her heart beat fast.

'*Not* because I didn't want to stay. Because I wanted to stay too much.' She shook her head and felt tears well. She didn't care any more. She couldn't keep it in. Not with their baby growing in her belly. 'I love you, Leo. I fell in love with you so hard that it knocked me for six. I couldn't bear the thought of staying with you only until you grew bored and decided to take a new mistress, or a wife.'

Leo gave a groan that sounded like a man on death row being given a reprieve. He reached out and pulled Angel into him, wrapping his arms tight around her. A great big sob was coming up from deep down inside Angel, and the enormity of it all was hitting her. Leo pulled back, and was blurry in her eyes, and she felt his hands come to her face, thumbs already catching the tears that were falling.

'Oh, Angel, my sweet Angel, don't cry—please don't cry. You can't cry, because I need to hear you say what you just said again.'

Through her gulping sobs Angel got out, 'I...
love...you... Have done for ages...' She ended on
a wail. 'And I'm really happy I'm pregnant with
your baby.'

Leo wrapped his arms tight around her again,
and all he said was, 'So am I...so am I...'

When her crying turned to hiccups Leo led her
back to a chair and knelt down before her again,
and made sure she'd taken a drink of water. Angel
felt raw and open. As if her beating heart was
lying there between them, telling him how vulnerable she was. He'd said all sorts of things, and
patently he wasn't upset about her being pregnant,
but he hadn't said that he *cared* for her...

'Angel, what you heard that day outside the
office—' Leo grimaced and looked shamefaced
'—was me being an absolute coward. The truth is
that the moment I saw you by the pool that night
I wanted you. And then afterwards, when I found
out who you were, and then saw you sneak into
the house...'

He tried to explain. 'I'd just decided to come
home to Athens, and the enormity of what our
family had been put through was still so fresh in
my head...and suddenly you were the enemy. It
changed everything.'

He shook his head. 'It's no excuse at all, but
when I thought you were about to walk away I re-

membered Dimitri Stephanides. I was determined to use anything I could to bind you to me. So I used Delphi and Stavros's marriage, completely misunderstanding the reason why it was so important to you.'

Leo caught her hand and kissed it. 'When Ari confronted me that day about you he caught a raw nerve. I was just realising that what I felt for you went so much deeper than desire. My whole life I've blocked out emotions, avoided intimacy, terrified of my world falling apart the way it did when I was a kid. I couldn't articulate any of that to him, and when he was all protective of you I lashed out, because I was jealous. Jealous of him feeling like he had some right to protect you from me…'

Leo put his hands back around Angel's belly, and she covered his hands with hers. He looked up, his eyes blazing.

'My childhood fears were nothing compared to what it was like to contemplate trying to live without you. Angel, I love you, and I love this baby. And I want you to come home with me and marry me and be my wife.'

She opened her mouth but he stopped her, as if anticipating something.

'And it's not just because you're pregnant.' He bent his head and pressed a kiss to her belly. He looked up. 'It's because I can't live without you, and if you don't come back home with me then I'm going to move here to be with you, because I'm not leaving your side ever again.'

Angel bent forward and took Leo's face in her hands. Her heart was so full she felt it could burst. 'The evening you stepped out of that pool you stole my heart, and I haven't been the same since. Ask me again.'

'Only if you kiss me first... God, Angel, I've missed you so much.'

With her heart in her mouth, Angel bent forward and kissed Leo sweetly, tenderly, until he wrapped one hand around the back of her head and pulled her closer, and the kiss quickly developed into something else much hotter.

Breathless, Angel pulled back. 'Ask me again.'

Leo's eyes burned, and his hand on her belly was like a brand. 'Angel, will you marry me? Because I love you more than life itself and quite simply can't function without you.'

'Yes, Leo, I will, and I want to go home with you.' Angel thought of something then, a dark cloud on the horizon. She bit her lip and Leo, immediately concerned, said, 'What is it?'

Angel's hands tightened on Leo's. 'Your father...he must hate me. He can't possibly welcome this.'

Leo smiled. 'Do you know that I always

assumed my father had chosen Olympia to be his bride out of logic and respect, a reaction to my mother's histrionics? It was the one thing I admired him for, and the reason I always thought I'd be able to stay away from messy emotions. But I was wrong. He loves Olympia, he never loved my mother, and that was the problem. I never saw that, though, until recently. He's an old man, he's got his lifelong wish to be at home. He's quite happy to bury any ill feeling between our families, and certainly doesn't hold you responsible.'

Relief burst through Angel, but even so she said, 'You're not just saying that?'

Leo smiled. 'No, I'm not just saying that. Now, can we get out of here and go home?'

'Yes, please.' Angel stood up and let Leo help her into her coat. The Irish early autumn weather was making itself felt, with rain starting to spatter and grey clouds rolling overhead when they walked outside.

Angel tugged on Leo's hand and pointed over to where the gothic abbey sat. She glanced at him shyly, and Leo felt his heart expand so much he nearly couldn't contain it.

'When I was at school here I used to imagine that a handsome prince would come and rescue me and take me home.'

Leo turned Angel to face him and wrapped his

coat around her, pulling her in close. Her head was tipped back and he could feel the burgeoning swell of her belly digging into him. *Their baby.* They were a family now.

Leo's voice was husky. 'Well, if you don't mind your prince coming a little late, and still kicking the clay off his feet, I'd like to rescue you and take you home.'

Angel smiled tremulously. 'I wouldn't settle for anyone else.'

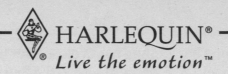

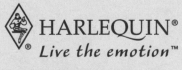

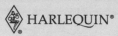

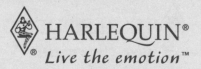

HARLEQUIN®
INTRIGUE®

BREATHTAKING ROMANTIC SUSPENSE

Shared dangers and passions lead to electrifying
romance and heart-stopping suspense!

Every month, you'll meet six new heroes
who are guaranteed to make your spine tingle
and your pulse pound. With them you'll enter
into the exciting world of Harlequin Intrigue—
where your life is on the line
and so is your heart!

THAT'S INTRIGUE—
ROMANTIC SUSPENSE
AT ITS BEST!

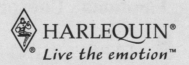

...there's more to the story!

Superromance.
A *big* satisfying read about unforgettable characters. Each month we offer *six* very different stories that range from family drama to adventure and mystery, from highly emotional stories to romantic comedies—and much more! Stories about people you'll believe in and care about. Stories too compelling to put down....

Our authors are among today's *best* romance writers. You'll find familiar names and talented newcomers. Many of them are award winners—and you'll see why!

If you want the biggest and best in romance fiction, you'll get it from Superromance!

Exciting, Emotional, Unexpected...

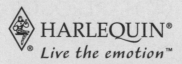

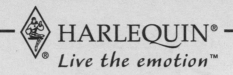